Henry VIII and His Six Wives

Henry's voice was thick with rage. 'I can trust no one. You all play me false.'

Katherine rose unsteadily. 'Do I?' she asked. 'Did I at Flodden?'

"Ha! I knew you would throw that at my head. You did not beat the Scots, Madam—you may have addressed the troops, but Flodden was won by the Howards, by English halberds. And you would do well to attribute your victories to God, my lady, before yourself. You think to rule me, but you would do well to assume a woman's role and give me a child, an heir to the throne.'

'Do you think I don't pray for that? Each day of my life?' she stammered.

'One stillborn female hidden away like a pauper's brat—two boys that cannot live out a month——'

'Sir, if you have any love for me——'

'Princes do not marry for love, Madam, but to beget children.'

ACCLAIM FOR THE FILM

". . . excellent moments to be savoured . . ."
—*Daily Express*

"This is a real film, made by a director who will always try for something better than the obvious."
—*The Guardian*

". . . I can't imagine it being done better . . ."
—*Evening Standard*

". . . the film's success at suggesting wilful magnificence shows how much experience can be crammed into one body, never mind one reign."
—*Evening Standard*

". . . an exhilarating surprise."
—*Sunday Telegraph*

"It is a vivid, literate film . . ."
—*Films Illustrated*

Keith Michell "is magnificent—unsurpassable."
—Espeth Grant, *Tatler*

HENRY VIII AND HIS SIX WIVES

Maurine Peters

BALLANTINE BOOKS • NEW YORK
An Intext Publisher

SBN 345-02817-1-125

This edition published by arrangement with
Fontana Books.

First Printing: September, 1972

Printed in the United States of America

BALLANTINE BOOKS, INC.
101 Fifth Avenue, New York, N.Y. 10003

❉❉ CONTENTS ❉❉

PROLOGUE

The long Tudor day was done, and night hung like a pall over Hampton Court. Under its blackness, within the corridors and rooms lit by soaring tapers, men and women moved, whispering, their shadows thin and flat like echoes of themselves against the walls. They were accustomed to their own mortality. These ladies with jewels winking on breasts and fingers, these gentlemen in their fur-collared doublets, had all witnessed the end of a life before, and knew it would happen to each one of them.

But this was not a little death. England herself groaned and gasped upon the high, canopied bed, in the bloated, corrupted mass of stinking flesh who was still King Henry the Eighth, Sovereign Lord, until the last breath forced itself between clenched and rotting teeth. When the last breath was exhaled, England herself would change, and memory would begin to fade.

So many memories! The room was full of them, writhing and twisting up the shadowed tapestries. The King sighed, for some memories were worse than the blisterings and purgings with which the physicians had sought to draw the poisons out of his leg. He could see the doctors now, huddled close like naughty schoolboys.

A little apart from them the members of his Council muttered together. He wanted to call to them to speak up, to remember it could be construed as treason to exchange secrets before a King; but his voice faded into a small groan and a spasm of pain cramped his limbs.

He must have made some sound, for the Queen's

eyes turned towards him with a softly pitying look. She knelt at the foot of the bed with her small, plump hands folded under her round chin, and next to her, his daughter, Mary, wept in the snuffling manner that always irritated him. When she was little she had never cried, but she had shed many tears since then.

One of the Council had approached the bed and knelt, mouth close to the King's ear. The thin, bearded face bore a fleeting likeness to poor, dead Jane. It hurt the King to recognise the traces of his best-loved wife in the lineaments of Edward Seymour, her brother, almost as if the latter had committed some breach of taste.

Seymour's words issued in a little gush, as if he had learned them by heart and feared he might forget them.

'Your Grace must prepare to meet his God.'

It took courage to tell a monarch that he must die, for the words themselves were technically treason.

The King heard his own voice, tinged faintly with sarcasm.

'What judge sends you to pass this sentence?'

'Your physicians, sir. They can do no more. It is time for Your Grace to weigh his past life—and seek for God's mercy through Christ.'

Edward Seymour's voice broke a little on the last words, as if he unconsciously relished the pathos of the moment.

They were all looking towards the bed now, like children waiting for something to happen. But nothing, thought the King with a surge of anger, is going to happen to *them*! They will be here when they proclaim my son and I will be—*where*? Locked in stone beneath the earth, hammering upon my carved coffin lid to be set free again to enjoy the scents and sights of a world I am not ready to leave. Fifty-six is not old, not in these times when men can live into their seventies. I am still young though these fools cannot see it!

His eyes roamed the grave and tearful faces, but others crowded from the tapestries, laughing and cheering before him. He knew those London faces, had heard them shout, 'Hurrah for Prince Hal! God bless King Henry!' The crowds loved him, more than they had loved his miserly father or the gentle Arthur who had had the tact to die young and leave the throne vacant for his lusty younger brother. Aye, lusty was the word, and never more so than in the tiltyard.

A freshening breeze swept through the close-packed stands, fluttering the light veils of the women, swirling dust from between the paving stones. Sunshine glinted on the ring suspended in the centre of the yard and on the glittering lance raised to catch the target upon its point. The lance slid past the circle as the rider mistimed his thrust, and above the roar of the crowd a trumpet shrilled, high and sweet.

Another rider left the barrier, and thundered down upon the prize. No rotting hulk with swollen hands plucking the covers, but a golden lad, peach-cheeked and sapling-straight.

'The King has it! A hit! A hit!'

The horse shuddered, turning its haunches in obedience to the tightened reins as the victor acknowledged the shouts. Then he turned again towards the royal stand, riding across the space with his eyes on the young woman who sat, her face glowing proudly, as he dipped the lance and let the ring fall into her silken lap.

'For our son, Madam. For the Prince.'

His voice was a joyous pledge of the love he felt for his Spanish wife, for Katherine of Aragon, who had been a virgin and his brother's widow when he married her, so that he valued her the more on that account, just as he cherished his crown because it had originally been intended for Arthur.

The Queen had given him a son, proof of his virility, a future monarch for the land wrested from a Plantagenet grasp. They knelt together now at High Mass, their heads bowed in thanksgiving as the choir chanted the *Te Deum* and the pungent incense clouded the gold-tinged candlelight.

And later, when God had been duly thanked, in the great hall of Westminster, Henry had sat, robed in purple next to his fruitful Spanish wife, and watched the pageant devised so cleverly to delight the Court and those citizens who had been admitted to the occasion.

It was to honour the Queen too, for she had been the vessel that received and bore the royal seed, and so above the decorated float the initial 'K' was twined with the initial 'H'; and among the roses of York and Lancaster the Queen's pomegranates glimmered against leaves of green velvet stitched with silver thread.

Such a subtle fruit, the pomegranate, yielding its sweetness drop by drop with the pricking of a pin; and Katherine had been young then and a mother for the first time. There had been a harmony in her words and gestures that day, and the air around had been full of laughter. Laughter, and good-fellowship, and the tender glance of a fruitful wife—those things had meant so much to him.

Now, desperately, in these last moments, as memories crowded the shadowed room, he sought to evade the cold clutch of death.

THE TIME OF THE POMEGRANATE

❉❉❉

❉❉ CHAPTER ONE ❉❉

Henry dug his spoon into a red dragon jelly and conveyed the quivering morsel to his mouth. It was sweet on his tongue with a hint of cloves, and blended with the Rhenish he had drunk. Further down the high table Bishop Fisher applauded the richly decorated float with childlike delight. The Bishop, for all his intellectual acuteness, had about him a disarming innocence of manner. It was shared to a great extent by the pleasant-faced man who sat nearer the King. A cultured being, this Thomas More, and a good father to his children.

Henry, congratulating himself on having recognised the value of this unassuming lawyer, leaned over to say cordially,

'Thomas, I hear you educated your wife—will you do the same for my boy?'

'Gladly, sir.' More spoke promptly with a brief, unemphatic nod of the head.

'Would you?' Delighted by the lack of hesitation, Henry swung round to Katherine who placidly nibbled a sugar-plum with her mind, no doubt, far away in the nursery at Richmond, for she gave a little jump as he cried, 'Catalina, my love, did you hear? More's going to educate the Prince!'

'An honour, Your Grace.' She was instantly attentive, her rather harshly accented voice warm with pleasure.

'What would Your Grace have him learn?' the Bishop enquired.

'Everything!' Henry exclaimed. 'The old and the new. Duns Scotus, Euripides, your Erasmus——'

'Sir, at this moment the ladies are waiting for you to celebrate his *birth*!'

The courtier who had leapt up to the daïs was a beefily handsome young man, almost as tall as the King and possessed, like him, of an animal vitality. Beside Charles Brandon, More and Fisher seemed pale and serious, out of tune with the mood of the afternoon.

Henry spat into the white napkin held up before him by a page and excused himself in an abstracted manner that proclaimed a shift of interest from his heir's scholastic training to the pleasure of the moment.

He was, thought Katherine fondly, no more than a great boy himself, for all his philosophising with scholars like More and Fisher. As he capered and leapt among the dancers, his eyes sought the admiration in her face. He must out-dance, out-run, out-shoot them all, and she must be the loving satellite to his splendid sun.

The Bishop, eyeing the King's companions with less than wholehearted approval, allowed himself to be faintly peevish.

'The only text Brandon ever read would be a stud-book.'

'Charity, my lord.'

More gave his quizzical grin and turned his attention to the dancers again as they whirled and flashed, with the golden initials spinning from their tunics. Feet tapped in time to the plucking of the harp strings and the invited citizens pressed about the decorated float, their fingers itching towards the golden pomegranates.

The music ended at a signal from the King and Henry's voice rang out clearly.

'Largesse to the commons!'

All must share in the triumph of his loins. His subjects must be permitted to strip the float, to deck themselves in the garlands of silver, to stuff their breeches with the winking jewels. And Henry himself, tearing a golden 'H' from his costume, presented it to the smiling Queen and turned, arms wide, to his Court.

'Come! You shall pick them from me!'

And then, like a mischievous schoolboy, he nimbly danced and dodged as twenty hands reached out to strip him of his finery. There was a wild, sweet madness among them all now. Commoners and courtiers mixed and mingled, ripping the silk from knightly backs, tearing at lace coifs and jewelled collars, reaching out for the gilded hangings, the encrusted salt-cellars upon the table.

The guards clanked forward unevenly, their expressions wary, but Henry, stripped to his underclothes, waved them away, and, one arm around Brandon's shoulder, pointed gleefully to a perspiring gentleman who clung to the branches of an artificial tree, vainly trying to extricate himself from the clutching hands of the mob who had already divested him of every stitch of clothing.

Even the Queen's grave Spanish composure had melted into delighted laughter. She too was leaning forward in her seat, applauding and encouraging. The dark-cloaked messenger who had threaded his way to her side had to repeat his whispered sentence before she turned and stared at him, with all the laughter dying in her face so that she looked suddenly all of her six years seniority to the King.

Katherine left her place at once, walking carefully as if the broken flowers strewn over the floor would cry out in pain if she trod upon their jewelled petals, and she folded her arms about herself as if she too might break at a touch.

Henry, laughing still, heard her coldly controlled voice.

'Henry. *Escuchame! Tenemos que irnos a* Richmond.'

He saw her through a haze of wine and goodwill, and would have swept her into the circle of his arm, but she was looking at him with an expression that made a mockery of the rejoicing and her voice was almost ugly as she spoke, in English this time.

'We must go to Richmond. *Now.*'

He could see the lights of Westminster flaring into the soft twilight as the royal barge was rowed swiftly upriver. Then he turned his back and strained his eyes through the gloom ahead while his thoughts sped more quickly than the rowers to the palace of Richmond.

It had been his mother's favourite residence, named originally Shene, but retitled by his father. A pleasant place, green and plague-free, with gardens where a small boy could chase a ball or romp with a puppy.

The message had been garbled. No doubt there was a mistake somewhere and the baby had had no more than an attack of colic. Nurses were always apt to panic, especially if their charge were royal. He wanted to tell Katherine that, but when he glanced towards her she was looking down at her hands, as if she were learning the lines upon them by heart; and he couldn't think of anything to say.

At the main door of the palace servants knelt at the royal approach, and the news was in their faces even before the physicians drew him aside. He heard them as if they spoke from a great distance and the stairs beneath his feet were insubstantial, as though he walked through a dream.

The nurse was weeping and he envied her the easy moisture that flowed from beneath her reddened lids. There was a great weight pressing down upon his own heart and a tightness in his throat that made it difficult to speak.

Katherine was standing by the carved and gilded

cradle, her face shadowed by her hood. He watched her put out her hand and touch the small, shrouded bundle in a blind, groping gesture. Then she turned her head aside and stood, with bowed shoulders, as if she had just suffered a terrible defeat.

Something broke in the King then, and he went to her swiftly, pressing her face into his chest, saying her name over and over. But when he looked into her eyes, they were dry and her voice was heavy with guilt.

'I was not here,' she said, numbly.

He held her more closely as words of useless comfort poured out of him.

'There was no remedy, nothing the physicians could do. It was too sudden. Kate—it was the will of God.'

'The will of God,' she whispered.

'And we must accept it.' He forced himself to believe in his own words, feeling her tremble against him.

'The will of God,' she repeated dully.

'We must ask His blessing,' Henry urged. 'We will make pilgrimage again—to Hailes, Walsingham. Kate, we are both young. We can have other children. God has chosen to take the boy, but we——'

It was impossible to continue. Her shaking misery tarnished his own noble acceptance. He sank to his knees, the King of England acknowledging the King of Heaven, and some quality in him stirred Katherine to cry out, in anguish.

'I will give you an heir. I promise you.'

It is in the bearing of healthy sons that a wife proves her value. I have lost a child, but Henry has lost a successor. We are not private people grieving for a dead babe, but monarchs of a royal line with crowns committed to our care. It is not for us to weep too long over the past, but to plan again for the future.

She knelt beside the King and her voice was steadier than his as she raised it, imploring, to Heaven.

It was easier for a man to forget, for men had duties and obligations to perform. Women must sit and sew, or chatter with their ladies, or smile at the amusements devised by their husbands. But a King could go into his Council chamber and shut out his private self. What pleased Katherine more than any masques or banquets Henry planned was that, after the discussions behind closed doors, he would tell her about them and ask for her opinion as if she were important to him for other reasons besides her sex.

But there were times in Council when the King's patience wore thin. There were times when his fist clenched upon the arm of his chair and the vein in his temple swelled as he listened to his older advisers mumble against his plans. On this particular day it was Warham, Archbishop of Canterbury, who quavered, white-haired and venerable.

'Sir, your father's policy was ever to avoid war. Aside from the financial consideration of sending forty thousand men into France——'

'And you talk just like my father,' Henry interrupted, pleased with the smiles that flitted over the faces of his companions.

Most of them could recall only too clearly the mournful face and voice of King Henry the Seventh as Warham droned, 'But how much will it *cost*?'

'Now the Archbishop will tell me that God only permits war because of our sins,' Henry said, in jocular fashion.

'Your Grace, I——' Warham looked unhappy and confused, twisting the seal ring on his finger.

'My quarrel is God's quarrel, isn't it?' Henry snapped.

Bishop Fisher said in his gentle, tactful way, 'Sir, all the world knows Your Grace's zeal in the Pope's cause and that you would rather die than take any dishonour —the point in question——'

'The point in question, my tutor, is whether we allow the King of France, a pronounced heretic, to bend all Christian princes to his will and pleasure!'

The King's irritation exploded into a sharp, sudden rage. He had nothing against poor old Fisher but it was time the Bishop realised that he, Henry, was no longer in the schoolroom.

'My lords, we are in a holy league with the Emperor and his Spanish Majesty to defend Christendom—are we to betray our sworn alliance?' the King demanded.

Henry paused, catching Lord Howard's muttered, 'The Queen's been at him.'

It was so near the truth that he decided to ignore the remark.

'And France is mine by inheritance,' he flashed out.

He grinned round at them triumphantly, wondering if anyone would dare to dispute the fact. Archbishop Warham, looking more than ever like a startled, ageing rabbit, twitched nervously and spoke as if he were feeling his way carefully.

'True, but Your Grace must know that French conquest has never served to enrich the Kingdom.'

That was all they ever thought about, these old men with ink in their veins instead of red blood. And here was Lord Howard's father, biting his underlip as he asked, 'What levy would need to be raised?'

'A tenth.' Bishop Fox glanced up from the documents in front of him.

'The commons won't like that,' Fisher warned.

'I don't like it,' old Howard grumbled. 'I'm not against giving the French a good hiding—God knows they've earned it—but what surety have we that our men won't come limping home with the flux again?'

Young Howard answered smartly, a teasing look about his mouth.

'Because Master Almoner will see this time that they

have proper victuals.'

'Can you do that, Master Wolsey?'

Old Howard fired his question the length of the table to the man who had listened silently, his eyes hooded between their folds of skin. The newest member of the Council, the son of a butcher now seated among aristocrats of gentle descent, he surveyed them with apparent indifference.

'Can you procure good, cut-rate beef for us, Master Wolsey?' Howard gibed.

Henry led the roars of laughter that swept the company. It was Fisher who brought the subject back to graver, political matters.

'My lords, we have not yet considered the other danger—Scotland. With so many men out of the Kingdom they might do us great mischief.'

There was a general nodding of heads. The Scots were always up to mischief, for all that King James had wed Henry's own sister, Margaret. A full-scale invasion from the north would be dangerous with so many from home, and Scotland was traditionally an ally of France.

'Sir, Fisher's right,' Warham said quickly. 'With all respect to Your Highness, I propose that we wait upon events. If there should be a change of fortune, if the Emperor should prevail——'

Wolsey spoke for the first time, his deeper voice cutting across the Archbishop's quieter tone.

'By your leave, sir—would it not be a sorry thing for His Grace, being so expert in archery, to see the Emperor with more strings to his bow?'

Henry, purpling with pleasure, shot out a forefinger in acknowledgment. Trust Master Wolsey to get at the heart of the matter! Why should the Emperor Maximilian win all the glory of a French campaign while a younger, lustier monarch cowered at home, counting pennies and defending his borders against the Scots?

A heated discussion began in the midst of which Warham's voice sounded a plaintive note.

'Sir, I beg you not to be led into any foolishness.'

So they called it foolishness, to honour one's treaties, to march out against a heretic King, to seek to recapture some of the possessions that were rightfully his by descent and ancient conquest.

The King's eyes narrowed slightly as he listened to the babble, and then his voice rang out, silencing them.

'My lords, I have ever accepted your good counsel, but in this instance I do overrule you. The dignity and estate of the Roman Church must be defended.'

And let old Warham and Fisher object to that motive if either of them dares. As far prospective trouble from Scotland—he raised his voice again.

'The Queen, as Regent, will hold something of our power at home, while I lead the army into France. Master Wolsey will furnish men, food, transport, and all our engines of war.'

The King had spoken and they might mutter and shake their heads as gravely as they pleased, but there was nothing any of them could do. Katherine would be delighted to learn that he intended to honour the alliance he had made with her father, King Ferdinand, and with the Emperor, Maximilian.

She would be flattered by his making her Regent, for it would give the lie to those who whispered that he valued her less because she was childless. Not that she was barren! It was simply the will of God that she had not yet borne a healthy son.

This campaign might change matters, for if the King of England busied himself with God's affairs then it was only right and proper that God should interest Himself in the King's business.

He rose, waving a dismissal and smiling inwardly as they trooped out disconsolately. Master Wolsey was the last to leave, and his eyes approved the King's actions as he bowed. I have, thought Henry, with a certain complacency, chosen wisely when I recognised this man's talents. He will be most useful to me.

He yawned and stretched, the close air of the Council room making him long for a fresh breeze and a horse between his legs. He would ride with Brandon and then he would go to Katherine and tell her what had been decided. With God's grace, there would be a son in the royal cradle by the time he returned from France.

❉❉ CHAPTER TWO ❉❉

The preparations for war were almost as exciting as war itself, and Henry threw himself into them with all the enthusiasm of a hot-tempered young colt longing to kick up its heels in a new pasture. He wanted to be everywhere at once and generally succeeded in being in most places. Foundrymen, leather-aproned and sweating, would look up from the hissing metal of a newly-tempered cannon to see their monarch, his hand on Wolsey's shoulder.

'The image of St. Luke is stamped upon the barrel! Oh, the Queen must see this! She must see our apostles!'

Wolsey was always near the King these days. And Katherine was often with them, heavier now, with the lines clear in her face when she was trapped in a shaft of sunlight, but still eagerly admiring her husband's plans. A lovely lady, the Spanish Queen. So said the gunners and archers lined up in their ranks for inspection.

But when the rough Channel crossing was behind them and they marched in pouring rain along the muddy road that led to Thérouanne, they forgot the noble sweetness of the King's wife, and cursed as they struggled to keep the gun-carriages upright. It was all very well for the nobility who rode their great stallions with no regard for the filth they churned up. If they were captured they might expect a brief captivity and an honourable ransom, but devil take the foot-soldiers pressed into the mud like the scum they were!

Heaving at a proud cannon, now belly-flopped into the marsh, they heard the jingling of bells and peered up into the rain-plastered face of the King, who called down without ceremony, as if he were one of themselves.

'Which is it?'

Brandon answered, squinting at the dragged mass of metal.

'St. John, sir.'

The King shook raindrops from the brim of his flat hat and yelled into the wind.

'Pull at it! Thighs and muscles!'

His own hard muscles rippled under the drenched silk of his tunic.

'To Thérouanne!' he cried.

That was all, and he rode on, head lowered into the wind. But they risked a cheer before they bent their backs to the ropes again and the cannon was sucked up more easily because of the fresh heart in them.

Yet it was a relief to pitch camp on the outskirts of the town, to dig the ditches and shake the gravel from their boots, to oil their bows and check their powder anxiously. There was time now to pick a woman from among the camp-bawds, though the captains had first choice of the prettiest. And in the centre of the trodden field, the twin standards of Henry the Eighth and the Emperor Maximilian fluttered over the vast war-tent.

Within, flanked by a half-eaten dinner, the two rulers sat at their ease, the white hair and shrewd black eyes of the older man contrasting with the ruddy locks and fresh complexion of the other. It was Henry, setting down his wine goblet, who opened the conversation with the polite wariness of a man who is not certain how to gauge the mood or meaning of his companion.

'Your Highness——' His voice trailed away as his guest contradicted affably.

'Maximilian, please.'

'We could take Thérouanne today, sir,' Henry said eagerly. 'There's enough breaches in her.'

As if to underline his words the muffled boom of a cannon reverberated beyond the canvas. Maximilian stroked his short beard and cocked an eyebrow.

'And you would like to lead the attack in person, eh?' he enquired. 'My dear boy, you are delightful, a real warrior, but far too valuable to us all to risk such an action. The pheasant'—he broke off to savour a mouthful and then resumed, smiling—'is delicious. Ah! I could wish my grandson more like you. Poor Charles, it's very sad. He has adenoids.'

He pronounced the word with a delicate distaste that immediately conjured up a vision of the sallow youth born of the marriage between Maximilian's son and Katherine's unstable sister, Juana.

'Yes,' Maximilian continued brightly, 'I am almost tempted to resign and make you Emperor in my place.'

'You're flattering me,' Henry said uncertainly, but at the other's pouting shake of the head, he cried in a burst of generosity, 'When Thérouanne falls I insist that Your Highness accept this town as his own.'

'Very princely. I accept,' Maximilian said, with the frankness of gratitude in his smile.

'And you shall of course precede me with full honours at the entry,' Henry added.

'My dear boy, I wouldn't dream of it,' Maximilian said warmly. 'As I told you, I have come to serve under your banner like any other foot-soldier. All I ask are my expenses.' He paused, raising his goblet. Watching Henry's laughter jerk into silence, he added, 'A hundred crowns a day. My King—to your triumph!'

So the Austrian fox had outwitted the English hound. Henry's troops would have the honour of all the fighting while the Emperor collected his hundred crowns a day and claimed the town as a gift from his dear ally. Yet, one had to admire the man and at least the glory of the campaign would go to England's handsome young King.

It was not, despite the initial preparations, turning out to be much of a campaign after all. The French were noticeably reluctant to stand and fight, and their poorly defended towns opened their gates as if the English were heroes and not conquerors.

Henry, riding slowly down a narrow street, lifting his hand in acknowledgment of the cheers, thought that crowds in France were much the same as the English mob. There were the usual veterans of other battles with their eye patches and bandaged stumps, housewives with children clinging to their skirts and the scars of pox upon their faces, boys eager to share vicariously in the triumph of their elders, and young girls running forward with garlands of flowers to hang about the necks of the soldiers. So many young girls, their breasts high and firm, their hips slender, and in their bright eyes an invitation to a lonely man who had left an ageing, slack-bodied wife at home.

A thin-flanked maid, with her kirtle slit to the thigh and a mouth like a poppy, reached up brown arms to slip a garland about the King. Her lashes curved blackly above her high cheekbones and there was a sprinkling of freckles across her nose. Henry seized her around the waist and swung her behind him up to the high saddle where she clung, giggling, her face pressed into his mantle.

They camped within the town that night, circled by bonfires and the shouts of revellers, and Henry, armour laid aside, sang a song of his own composing while his fingers stroked the strings of the lute as if they were the curves of a woman's body. His tenor voice rose up into the haze of candlelight as tender and true as if it was never known to crackle with rage.

'The Rose will into France spring,
Almighty God him thither bring——'

He paused, eyes lowered to the instrument, and the assembled company joined in the final couplet:

'And save this flower which is our King,
This rose, this rose, this rose.'

And he had a rose of his own now that was sweeter and more exquisite than the flowers of the pomegranate. He could cup his hands at any time about the rounded softness of the pomegranate, but to strip the thorns from the rose and delve like a bee into its perfumed core—that made the little matter of the Emperor's wages unimportant.

Henry laid aside the lute and signalled for wine, lowering one eyelid in a sly wink as the girl with a mouth like a poppy came over and bent to refill his goblet, her buttocks round under the page's tunic in which she was now clad.

Later, on the crumpled bed, he took his pleasure of the rose, ripping away the tunic to reveal the thin brown back with the intriguing strawberry mark raised like a love-bite above the surrounding skin. This was the reward of campaigning and made the long marches through the rain and mud no more than the prelude to fulfilment.

In the Emperor's tent, Maximilian and Wolsey sat together, warming their hands at the brazier, their voices muted.

'But there's no opposition, Your Highness,' Wolsey was saying. 'They have no reserves.'

'Too late, too late.' The Emperor intoned the words mournfully. 'If we tried to take Paris now, it would mean a winter campaign. Very expensive that. Why be impatient? Your young King has shown his mettle. He has already taken one-two-three—five towns.'

He held up long fingers one by one, shielding his handsome old face from the light.

'All of which,' Wolsey murmured slyly, 'border Your Highness' territory.'

Maximilian gave him a long glance and shook his finger roguishly.

'His army has behaved superbly,' he commented. 'Also his almoner—who understands more than he professes, yes?'

Wolsey gave a slight bow and spoke with deliberate bluntness.

'You're making use of us, aren't you?'

'And I believe he realises why the French run rather than fight.' Maximilian flipped out his hand towards the Englishman. 'That a decisive battle would not be desirable, for either side. So—I think we take one more town before the season ends—the virgin city, they call it—incidentally the income of the bishopric there is quite considerable—and then begin again next year. Yes?'

They looked at each other with complete understanding, while in the crumpled bed yards away the King of England flung out a hand in contented slumber and covered a strawberry mark with his open palm.

So the game was continued for a little longer, with the emblemed cannons dragged through the mud, the priests and choir-boys chanting ahead of the steel-clad knights, the King raising his arm to bellow in an incoherence of excitement.

'On! On to Tournay!'

As the French flag was lowered on the ramparts of the castle, Henry rode through the gates in triumph, with the Emperor smiling modestly in the rear.

Later, they sat together on twin chairs raised on a daïs above the members of their Council. Before them, young Howard stood, reading aloud the letter with which he had arrived a half-hour before. His voice shook a little with excitement.

'Whereby, my husband, I send you this letter to tell you of the great victory that Our Lord hath sent your subjects in your absence. And for an earnest, Sir Thomas Howard brings you the King of Scotland's coat——'

With a conscious dramatic flourish, he waved forward a steward who flung down a tattered, bloodstained surcoat. There was a murmur of appreciative delight from the company.

'Go on, Howard. Go on,' Henry leaned forward and beamed.

Howard bent his attention to the letter again.

'I thought to send King James himself, sir, but our Englishmen would not suffer it. Therefore we would fain know your pleasure in burying Scotland's body. And with this I make an end, praying God to send you home shortly, for no joy can be accomplished here without you. Your humble wife and true servant, Katherine, the Queen.'

So the Scots had been driven back into their mountains and glens and their King lay dead. Katherine had proved a capable regent and Wolsey's advice had been sound. Unable to sit for a moment longer in dignified stillness, Henry leapt into the midst of them all to receive their congratulations.

They returned to cheers and crowded streets and to a Katherine so happy that one might have imagined her to have fought at Flodden herself, instead of merely sewing flags and banners for the standard-bearers to carry. Henry didn't grudge the Queen her triumph, but there were moments when he wished people would dwell a little less on the Scottish defeat and a little more on his French campaign. True, it had been inconclusive, but it would be renewed. Ferdinand of Spain was even now drawing up a new triple alliance, and next time Maximilian should bear a good part of the cost, for there was no denying that the treasury was woefully depleted.

The Queen was more contented than she had been for years. Not only did she have her husband back safely, but he was proud of her, listening to her advice, treating her as more than a spectator to the amusements he devised.

On the day that he sent for her, she hurried to his private chamber with eager anticipation. There had been an audience with the French ambassador earlier that day and Henry would be anxious to inform her of the details. At her side, Maria de Salinas, her favourite attendant, paced decorously. There was so little Maria didn't know of Katherine's heart, for they had been friends since childhood, had shared the years of loneliness and neglect after gentle Arthur's death.

The King was on his feet, a parchment crumpled in his hand. As the two ladies entered he turned a white set face in their direction and barked, with a jerk of his red head towards Maria.

'Send her out.'

Maria gave the Queen a startled, apprehensive glance, but Katherine's attention was fixed upon the tight mouth and blazing eyes of the King. As she curtsied and withdrew she heard the Queen's timid voice.

'Henry——'

'Don't speak, Madam. But read *that*.'

Henry flung the parchment on the desk between them and stood, glowering, as she smoothed it between her fingers.

'Is it your father's hand?' he demanded.

'Yes, but——'

'Read it!'

He threw the two words as if they were stones, and the writing on the parchment blurred before her eyes. She drew a deep breath to steady herself and read silently, hardly able to make sense of the meaning but so pressed down by her husband's anger that it seemed natural to slip to her knees, folding her hands tightly to stop their shaking.

'That was brought here by the French Ambassador,' Henry said. 'Proof that your father is a liar, Madam, a conspiring liar, and that he has made peace with France.'

'He must have reasons, sir——' she began, but he blazed down at her.

'Yes, he is to receive the territory of Navarre. He has been bribed, Madam, bought! Three months after promising to continue the war which he induced me to enter! As you induced me to it! Because I have been at some pains, Madam, some expense—and now, when we are ready to renew the campaign, when the Kingdom of France is at my feet, your father gulls me! And his servant the Emperor! Did you see this clause, Madam? Here, at the close? Speak it!'

He had thrust the document under her nose, so close that the words ran together. She could see the reddish hairs quivering along the backs of his hands. Her voice shook as she pronounced the syllables.

'"And if the King of England refuses to accept such a peace, we—the Emperor and I—do solemnly pledge ourselves to assist the King of France in the defence of his realm."'

'My friends! My sweet allies!' His voice was thick with rage. 'Oh, I see there is no faith in this world. I can trust no one. You all play me false.'

Katherine had risen unsteadily, holding to the desk for support, feeling the pain as its sharp edges rasped her hands.

'Do *I*?' she asked with deep reproach and flinched when he answered with a cruel brevity.

'Yes.'

'At Flodden?'

Even as she gathered her defences he crushed them with another outburst of rage.

'Ha! I knew you would throw that at my head. You did not beat the Scots, Madam—you may have addressed the troops, imagined yourself another Isabella, and sent me the King's coat in your vanity, but Flodden was won by the Howards, by English halberds. And you would do well to attribute your victories to God, my lady, before yourself. You think to rule me, but you would do well to assume a woman's role and give me a child, an heir to this throne.'

It was out at last. The thought that gnawed at him continually had been spoken.

'Do you think I don't pray for that? Each day of my life?' she stammered.

'One stillborn female hidden away like a pauper's brat—two boys that cannot live out a month——'

'Sir, if you have any love for me——'

Her lips could scarcely shape the words, but he bore down upon her, lashing with his tongue.

'Princes do not marry for love, Madam, but to beget children.'

Something proud and defiant rose up in her, something to combat her own guilt. A voice that no longer sounded like her own screamed back at him.

'Then give me a healthy child!'

They stared at each other in horror; then Katherine threw herself upon her knees again, her hands twisting the rich brocade of her dress.

'Sir, I am yours—your servant—I renounce Spain—I cannot think of my father without shame——' she sobbed.

Argue politics, discuss foreign affairs, apologise for the double-dealing of one's father, but never talk of private griefs again! Never look honestly at the emotions that drive you apart even though you are bound together in matrimony. It is best for a loving wife to hide the truth, even from herself.

The King spoke coldly, without looking at her.

'That is as well, Madam, for I intend making peace with France and a greater peace than your father can imagine. I've been made the royal fool! But I've learned the lesson and they shall never deceive me again.'

He moved away then and looked back at her, his voice indifferent to her misery.

'I shall never trust anybody any more,' he said flatly and left her kneeling there.

Only his picked advisers might be exempted. Men like Wolsey who had showed him that he was a powerful King, and Thomas More who recognised an affinity of intellect—these men understood his nature. They would carry out his wishes without presuming to correct or control him.

He shut Katherine out of his mind. The daughter of the Spanish King must learn that her place was in a bed, not at the Council table. She must bear him healthy sons, and not reproach him for something that was not his fault. Lord! but she would be astonished if she ever guessed at his lustiness. He thought with pleasure of little Mistress Blount who had been so sweetly yielding a few nights before. He might even get her with child, he decided, then none in the Court would be in any doubt as to who was to blame for the lack of an heir.

Meanwhile there was a peace treaty to be drawn up with France, and the money intended for campaign would be employed instead upon England's defences. He would command new dock-yards to be built at Deptford and Woolwich, and he would act upon Wolsey's suggestion that a guild of pilots be formed to examine the whole question of sounder navigation. He would fill the Channel with ships to protect the shores of his kingdom from the treachery of foreign allies.

So an expensive peace was concluded and the harbours of England echoed to the clanging of hammers and the shouts of men as they sawed the great logs felled in the green forests. As the Spanish wife prayed and grew a little older day by day, Henry sat with Wolsey in the gently rocking cabin of his latest and most modern ship.

Light reflected from the water below the port-hole dappled the walls and danced over the red robes of the newly-created Cardinal. The butcher's son had risen faster and higher than any man in the land, and his increased girth gave him an added dignity. He watched the King carefully, sensitive to the trend of his monarch's thoughts, but Henry was examining the panels in his new capacity as naval architect.

'She's well-built, but the timber's unseasoned. See to it, my lord. Draw up an enactment for the preservation of forests——'

'And the seeding of new ones?' Wolsey made a note on a jewelled tablet.

'Good. We have a moat about us, but it must be fortified.'

Wolsey inserted himself neatly into the conversational opening.

'If I may venture to say, sir—there are two further elements that constitute the defence of this kingdom. The love of your people, which Your Grace already has——'

Henry, eyes thoughtful, supplied the rest of the sentence. 'And a son—which I lack. Is that it?'

Wolsey spoke earnestly as if he were presenting a new idea to a reluctant listener.

'We must secure the succession, sir. Without it there could be a return to civil war. May I speak my mind?'

The King nodded slowly, his face intent.

'Are we so certain,' Wolsey asked, carefully, 'of the

legality of Your Grace's marriage? With his brother's wife?'

'There was Papal dispensation.'

The Pope had forgotten the tokens of virginity sent to him after Katherine's marriage to Arthur, but Katherine herself had always sworn that she had drawn blood from her heel with a knife to save Arthur from the shame of admitting his impotence.

'Could there be no objection to the dispensation?' Wolsey was asking. 'Did not Your Grace protest against the marriage, at your father's bidding, for political reasons?'

That had been old King Henry's sly cleverness. To keep the Spanish dowry by betrothing one son's widow to another son, and then making that other boy formally protest, lest at any time in the future a more profitable alliance might be negotiated.

'That was years ago,' Henry said moodily.

He had loved Katherine then, had wanted her because she had been his brother's widow. But weak and ailing, Arthur had never enjoyed her. At least that was what Katherine had always sworn, and how could a young bridegroom of eighteen summers know enough to contradict?

'As you are aware, sir, I have the greatest respect and admiration for the Queen,' Wolsey was continuing, 'but even in Rome they are saying Her Grace might be expected to step aside if there were no heirs, and that the Pope could not oppose a matter of such necessity to the State.'

'They expect it of me?' Henry spoke sadly. At that moment, he was the loving husband forced to put aside his private desires for the sake of the realm.

'May I remind Your Grace that there are precedents for annulment?' Wolsey urged. 'The King of France, King Henry of Castile——'

'No. Not yet.'

Henry had not meant to speak, but pictures of Katherine crowded suddenly into his mind. She had been pretty on their wedding night with her long fair hair streaming over her shoulders. He remembered how she had laughed when he had danced before her as Lord of Misrule on that first Christmas day after their marriage. She had worn a gown of silver tissue and her eyes had followed him adoringly as he leapt and capered among the other dancers.

Her joy in their first child had been so touching, and they had shared their grief at his untimely death. It would be needlessly cruel to cast her aside now. She was, after all, not much past thirty and in a soft light could still stir him to passion.

'I could not ask it of her yet,' Henry said more firmly.

'Of course, the Queen may still bear a living child,' Wolsey said smoothly. 'But should she not, Your Grace might do well to consider a Princess of France—for the safety of your nation.'

The Cardinal was right of course. Monarchs must marry in order to beget heirs, and if their wives prove barren they must be persuaded to step aside. But not yet—not yet. At least not until he loved someone sufficiently to make her his Queen in Katherine's place.

❉❉ CHAPTER THREE ❉❉

Days mounted into weeks and weeks rose into months and the years hurried on. There was a living child now, not the eagerly awaited male heir, but a fair-tressed girl with a soft complexion who chased butterflies in the gardens of Richmond, clapping her tiny hands together and gurgling with laughter as the bright-hued things flew away.

The elders watched her indulgently as they strolled about in the clipped grass. Katherine, who found it difficult to tear her eyes from her daughter, was relaxed and happy. It was so seldom they could enjoy a pleasant family afternoon free from the cares of state.

Henry was often kept from her by Council business these days. Even when he visited her he seemed preoccupied and ill-at-ease. She blamed the Cardinal for that. On outwardly cordial terms with the well-fed, red-robed figure, there was never a moment when she forgot the rumour that Wolsey had sought to persuade the King to set her aside in favour of some younger princess.

Mary's birth had changed all that, for the princess was healthy and likely to grow to adulthood. Henry had been so proud at her birth. He had lifted the swaddled babe in his arms and cried out to the Court.

'Now, by God's Grace, sons will follow.'

God had not granted them yet, but there was time enough. She was still young enough, though the last miscarriage had tired her somewhat so that she seldom danced now or rode to hounds. But she had her pledge against the future. If there were no sons, Mary would be Queen one day. If there were no sons . . .

The princess, clutching vainly at a darting, scarlet blur, ran past her nurse into her mother's arms. Katherine laughed over the bright head to where Thomas More stood.

'She simply cannot resist them,' she apologised, wondering what had brought the shadow into their friend's eyes.

'Such a little girl to catch a falling star!' was all that he said.

She thought she must have imagined the shadow, for a moment later he was laughing at one of the King's jokes.

It was such a happy afternoon that whenever Katherine wanted to recall the contented times she had only to close her eyes to conjure up the picture of them all, walking at their ease among the bright, skimming butterflies.

The King spent a lot of time with Thomas More in the latter's pleasant Chelsea home. There was little formality there, only good wine and food and the best conversation in London. It pleased Henry to hear the lively banter that went on between More and his daughters, and it gave him a curious little stab of envy when More teased his wife. When Henry attempted to tease Katherine she turned hurt, anxious eyes towards him as if she were trying desperately to find the malice behind the jest.

Thomas More was a man without malice, though his talk was spiced with wit and his mind, like a finely cut diamond, caught and reflected the diverse interests in which he spent his leisure. One of these was the fashionable science of astronomy which he related to the arts of philosophy and religion in a way that fascinated the King. They were like two boys as they peered through the telescope set up on the roof of More's house.

'Such a diversity of stars and planets—and that they

should all revolve around us!' Henry marvelled.

'Your Grace, there is a new theory that we are not the centre of things,' More said eagerly.

'Not!' Henry took his eye from the telescope and stared at his host.

'No, sir, but one of those planets. And we, too, revolve about the sun. Twenty-four circles,' More said whimsically, 'now serve to explain the entire universe.'

'How ordered it all is! How tuned—if we could be so ordered!' Henry gazed up at the dark, star-studded sky and asked, 'Do you hold with this theory?'

'I incline to it,' More admitted.

'Thomas—when I was a boy you were one of my heroes, the great name among scholars,' Henry said impulsively. 'It was always, "More says this, More thinks that." The years have not changed my feeling for you. Will you sit on my Council now, and advise me? I need your advice.'

'Then Your Grace shall have it—so long as I can keep a good conscience,' More said.

'What do you mean by that?' Used to having his offers accepted with flattering gratitude, Henry frowned slightly.

'That I may be allowed to serve God first,' More said soberly.

'Why, we all must.'

From beneath their feet the sounds of muffled laughter drifted up to them.

'Your family are late to bed,' Henry said, seizing upon the opportunity to change the subject, to lighten the strain that had crept into the atmosphere.

'They forget time when they chatter,' More said indulgently.

'Yes.' Henry listened for a moment and then asked sharply, 'What age is he? Your boy?'

'Nine, sir.'

'Well-favoured—strong, isn't he?' At More's nod,

Henry said, 'The Queen is expecting another child.'

'I am glad for you, sir.'

'At my Coronation you promised me sons and grandsons,' Henry said in an accusing voice.

'Yes,' More said warily.

'All the world has a son,' the King said with a dull and heavy resentment. 'Thomas—is my marriage impure? Is it accursed of God?'

Had he enquired of Wolsey, the answer would have been tactful and temporising, but More said with a gentle firmness that betrayed he had been considering the situation already,

'No, Your Grace.'

'Then why have I no boy?' Henry's voice trembled with rage and bewilderment held in check. 'Am I not a man? Am I not a man like you?' His fists clenched and he breathed deeply as he sought to cage his wrath. After a moment he said hoarsely, 'There is a verse in Leviticus that says no union contracted with a brother's wife may bear true issue. If this should again come to nothing—what should I do then?'

'Sir, I am no fit counsel in these matters.'

More felt a trembling uneasiness in his stomach as he answered, for at the back of the question lay the conscience of the King, and Henry's conscience marched with Henry's desires.

'You favour the Queen, I think.' It was impossible to tell if regret or unwilling approval were implicit in the words.

More risked a smile and a little apologetic shrug.

'Well, we will make a pilgrimage to the Abbey and seek God's blessing.' Henry gave a small, disappointed sigh and then essayed a little joke as feeble compensation for the sour turn the evening had taken. 'Who doesn't tremble when he considers how to deal with his wife?'

More's answering laugh was a forced one. In his

mind the sweet, ageing face of the Queen was too clear for comfort.

So they made pilgrimage. Henry in plain trunks and tunic knelt, cap in hand, before the cowled monks, while Katherine at his side gave her little, gracious inclination of the head as the Abbot bowed the knee, welcoming them as supplicants for the mercy of God. At the altar they knelt again, touching the wooden image of the Virgin, bowing their heads below the Abbot's prayers.

'Domine Deus, Omnium Creator, fortis et terrabilis, qui gloriosae Virginis Mariae corpus et animam, ut dignum Filu tui habitaculum effici mereretur, spiritu sancto cooperante praeparasti——'

Year after year, for fifteen years, coming to the altar to kneel on the harsh stone and pray for the son that never came, to cry out to Heaven against those little stillborn bodies. Time shrank until every pilgrimage became one occasion and Katherine aged in an hour from still fruitful maturity to a barren old age. The juice of the pomegranate was all sucked dry and lesser loves had faded and gone, and a white falcon rose screaming into the sky.

He had noticed her first at Hever though he had surely seen her before about her duties in the Court. Her sister, Mary, had been a plumply pretty armful, her brother, George, a gay and elegant companion in the chase. It was incredible that he could have seen her, spoken to her, touched her hand in the dance and not known that leap of the pulses, that singing desire between the thighs.

And then he had ridden to Hever Castle and she had sped across the garden into the sunlight and it was as if he himself had stood in shadow for many years. Was it perhaps in the uncertainty of the chase that the glamour of hunting lay? And when the long sport came to an end what would he find between his hands?

A thin, sallow girl, already into her late twenties and still unwed. A flat-breasted, boy-buttocked woman with an extra finger on one hand and a skin that glowed golden as if she held perpetual buttercups under her chin. A witch-haired, slant-eyed beauty with a husky voice that tore the soul out of his body with desire.

Nan Bullen, his Nan! And yet not his, for she twisted and turned, beating her wings in the empty air, swooping to peck at his cheek and soaring up again, leaving him earthbound, unsatisfied, tied to a heavy-faced woman with milkless breasts and an empty womb.

It was not Katherine's fault that of her many children only the Princess Mary had lived. Henry never blamed her for that but he did blame her most bitterly for refusing to acknowledge the truth that she had been his brother Arthur's true wife. In refusing to admit this she set herself up against the just punishment of God, displaying such obstinacy that there were times when he longed to take her by the shoulders and shake her until her teeth rattled.

'I will give you anything you desire, if only you will set me free,' he had pleaded.

'I cannot release what is bound to me by the laws of God,' she answered, and her eyes begged him to understand. He had had a little dog once that had run mad on a hot summer's afternoon so that it had had to be put down lest it bite anybody, and just as it died it had looked at him as his wife looked at him now. And even while pitying the animal he had hated it for dying too slowly, for gazing at him as if he were to blame.

'Mary shall not be called bastard, like the lad you fathered on Mistress Blount,' the Queen's harsh, tired voice had continued. 'Mary is no Richmond to bear the bend sinister upon her shield.'

'Neither is she a male, to sit upon a throne!'

'Queens have ruled alone before,' she flashed.

'Not in England, Madam! The only one who tried it was the Empress Matilda, and her cousin, Stephen, was swift to put her in her place!'

'As you seek to put me in mine?'

'I would have you honoured as the Dowager-Princess of Wales.'

'I am Queen of England and your lawful wife!'

It had ended, as it always ended, with Henry in a towering rage and Katherine tearfully obstinate. He had flung out to seek comfort in the Lady Anne's apartments and found her, laughing and bold, with her black head arched on the thin brown throat, and the gentlemen standing around, catching each honeyed word, each gurgle of mirth.

Younger, smarter, gayer people than the friends he and Katherine had shared, they clustered like moths about the sharp Bullen flame. He liked them all—Norris, Weston, Tom Wyatt; her brother George. He needed their good-fellowship, but most of all he needed Anne to lie quiet in his arms, to give him an heir.

An heir was a monarch's most important possession, for life was uncertain even for a healthy man and death could strike suddenly, even in the midst of good fellowship.

There had been that afternoon in the tiltyard at Westminster when the King had jousted with Charles Brandon, Duke of Suffolk. A friendly match had almost ended in tragedy, for as Henry galloped down the course he had realised too late the meaning of Howard's frantic signals.

The upper part of his visor was still open and there was no time to adjust it, no time to swerve, only time to pray swift as lightning that Suffolk's lance would miss its mark. The lance splintered against the helmet and there was the blur of his opponent's horrified eyes, the reeling grass, the tilting sky, and a sick, jarring pain in his head.

There must be an heir, to guard against the likelihood of future accidents but, before there could be a child, Anne must learn to yield. And Anne had fled back to Hever, taking all gaiety with her. He had written, begged, pleaded, sent rich gifts, gone in person to plead his cause, and she had cried out that she was not a Bessie Blount nor even her own sister, and he had promised on his oath that he intended honourable marriage and was sending to Rome to obtain an annulment of his marriage.

But the Pope would not yield. He was too frightened of Katherine's nephew, of the adenoidal Charles who was now Holy Roman Emperor in his grandfather's stead. The most the Pope had done was to send Campeggio to hear both sides of the case, but the old man shuddered with ague and groaned with gout, and behaved as if the lapse of years were of small importance.

And Wolsey! When the King thought of the Cardinal he felt a literal swelling in his heart as if poison festered there. Wolsey had been eager for annulment as long as the King planned to wed a French princess, but it was amazing how his enthusiasm had died when he learned the object of Henry's regard was the Bullen girl.

He had been Anne's enemy from the beginning, and for a time Henry had been torn between an old loyalty and a new desire. But if Wolsey had shown the King how to rule, so Anne could show him how to cast off old shackles and do what pleased him. And what pleased the King must necessarily please God, who had cursed a sinful union with a most plentiful lack of sons!

The King shifted, wondering if it were his fancy that the stone had grown harder and colder through the years. The Abbot had certainly aged, time marking deep furrows down his lean cheeks, his small eyes frostier than Henry remembered.

'*——ac sanctae generationi servetur, tibique in omnibus jugiter deserviat et vitam consequi mereatur aeternum.*'

The Abbot paused, glancing down at the bowed heads, made the sign of the cross in a wearily indifferent manner and concluded rapidly.

'*Per eundem Dominum nostrum Jesum Christum Filium tuum, qui tecum vivat et regnat in unitate ejusdem. Amen.*'

They crossed themselves sedately with downcast eyes, though the corners of Anne's mouth twitched slightly. She was aware that the Abbot considered her as the concubine, that it would give him and the few cowled monks, who bowed as they left, the greatest satisfaction to learn she had died in the plague or been thrown from her horse during the chase. At least they were politer than the market women who had pelted her litter with mud, crying shame upon her for a goggle-eyed whore. Yet she would swear that they envied her, for it was a fine thing to be desired by a King.

Once there had been a time when she had thought love could fill the whole world, but Harry Percy had been forbidden to see her and then another Henry had come, stirring her senses with diamond hearts and black velvet gowns. And always, always, just out of reach dangled the crown itself.

It took a subtle wit to promise and then deny, advance and withdraw, present a cool cheek instead of warm lips; but it served to hold the King's desire at fever-pitch. She, who had not been thought worthy of becoming Northumberland's daughter-in-law, would wear a crown.

But there were obstacles in the Pope, in the Cardinal, in the Queen—even, perhaps, in the King himself, who still entertained some affection for his wife. Katherine was at Hunsden with Princess Mary, and Anne knew jealously that Henry visited them occasionally.

She chased away the little fear, pushing back her hood and letting her black hair stream down over her neck and shoulders. As they emerged from the courtyard into the green of the surrounding woods her greyhound, Urian, bounded up, wagging his pleasure.

Anne bent to fondle the dog and Henry, signalling to Weston to bring his boots and hose, sat on the green turf, stretching his thick, muscled legs.

'Ah! To be able to breathe again!' Anne exclaimed, twisting in the green sunlight with her arms raised and her face turned up to the lacing branches.

'Was it cold in the Abbey, my lady?' Weston enquired.

'Frigid!' she shuddered. 'And those po-faced monks!'

'They forget obedience to their King,' Henry said. His voice rumbled a little in his chest and the gesture with which he summoned his page, young Tom Culpepper, was abrupt. Then his eyes fell upon Anne again and his mouth slackened a little with desire.

To compare his darting falcon with the woman the Pope called his lawful wife—but comparison was too cruel! Yet when he rode over to Hunsden to visit Katherine, she greeted him with such pleasure that for a moment the comely girl she had been looked out of her eyes, and he took her hand with more warmth than he had intended as they went indoors to the quiet room where their daughter sat.

The warmth faded a little as she bustled about, sending for fresh dishes to tempt him after his journey, talking nervously of Mary's progress at her music and the terror they felt at news of the London plague.

'So very good of Your Grace to allow Mary to come back from Ludlow and join me here! I am appalled by the number of deaths reported in the towns.'

Faded, thickened, she had lost her tranquillity as she poked a needle through the silk stretched across her embroidery frame and fumbled a little, stooping closer to the light.

'The fires must be kept banked,' Henry said, fighting down his irritation. 'They keep away infection.'

'And visitors.' Loneliness was implicit in the sad little phrase, but he gave her a brisk, 'Yes,' and swung round to his daughter.

Mary was too thin and pale, with the heavy eyes and compressed lips of one who has cried a lot. He shook off the twinge of guilt, reminding himself that she had been ill.

'Are you better now?' he asked cordially.

'Yes, father.' She fiddled with a bit of meat on her plate, sliding it up and down with the point of her knife.

'We can't have you taking ill,' Henry said cheerfully. 'When this is all over and you return again into Wales you must remember my prescriptions. Small but clean company, a little food, a very little wine, and above all the pills—by God, I've forgot them!—my Rasis pills!'

'The steward will bring them.' Katherine reached out towards the bell.

'Mary shall fetch them for me if she will,' Henry said. 'In the top of my cabinet.'

As she went, he unconsciously squared his shoulders. Sooner or later he must speak alone to his wife, but now that the opportunity had come, he found himself saying,

'The fewer people who touch the pills the better—

we don't know where it will strike next. Even Wolsey has it. But then he insisted on staying in London.'

'I think perhaps the Cardinal only pretends to have the sickness because you are angry with him,' Katherine said.

'They say the buriers won't touch the bodies now for fear of contagion, that they're left lying in the streets. It's a fearful time.'

He sat down by the fire, watching her as she freed her work from the frame and smoothed the silk. It was a man's shirt she made, and an uneasy tenderness welled up in him, only to be submerged in annoyance at her blind obstinacy and the uncanny knack she had of making him feel guilty.

She answered him in a low voice in which reproach and pleading were mingled.

'Fearful—and strange—that we must have the plague before you will come to stay here and dine with us.'

'Madam, as to visiting your apartments when I am not your lawful husband——' he blustered, but she cut him short indulgently as if he were a child.

'Yes, yes, we have heard all that.'

As she rose and came over to measure the shirt against him, he saw cruelly magnified the lines across her brow, the sagging cheeks, the grooves that indented deeply from nose to mouth. Only a strand of greying hair showed beneath her coif and her hands, absently patting the silk, had in them something of prayer.

Hopefully, glancing up at her, he enquired, 'You will not enter into religion, Madam?'

'No, sir.' She frowned at a wayward thread.

'Louis of France's wife withdrew into a convent when she was divorced from him,' Henry said.

'But we are not divorced.' She took the shirt and sat down again, raising her head to remark with a disconcerting gleam of humour. 'I will enter a convent, Henry, when you enter a monastery.'

'That might be arranged, Madam,' he said slowly.

'And now you are thinking that you could be absolved later from your vows,' she said calmly.

They had been married too long. She knew every twist and turn of his logic, and yet there was a great kindness in her face.

'Kate,' urgently, pleadingly, he begged, 'let me free.'

The obstinacy settled down over her features like a mask, and the hope died in him, even as she began to speak.

'Sir, you know that only the Pope can dispense justice in our case. If his court pronounces against me, you are free—and then perhaps I will enter a convent.'

He had heard it all before, over and over, until his jaws ached with the boredom of it. The truth was that she would never let him go. He would have to drag out the rest of his life with her shackled to him like a ball and chain.

Her voice droned on below the crackling of the fire. It was hot in the room and he had eaten too much dinner. There were times when a man wearied of argument and craved only the oblivion of sleep.

'I should like their rule of silence,' Katherine said thoughtfully. 'Yes—I know how much you wish it for me! But I will not dishonour my name, or our daughter's name. And yet I long for that peace I have never known since I left my own country.'

She had been sixteen, too well-schooled in the discipline of the Spanish Court to cry in public, but her throat had ached as her parents accompanied her up the gangplank of the ship that would bear her across treacherous seas to a fog-bound island where she would marry a boy she had never seen. They had been kind to her, those English crowds who flocked about her litter. The Spanish alliance was a popular one and the people had seen beneath the stiff, shy dignity to the frightened, homesick girl.

Such a brief marriage that was, in physical fact, no marriage at all, and then gentle Arthur had died and she was an unkissed widow, living out her days as a pensioner in the English Court.

'All those years,' she mused, 'when I was kept here like a poor relation waiting to see if you would marry me, eating thin food, turning hems until there was no material left to turn——'

Looking up, hoping for some word, an indulgent smile, she saw Henry had dozed off. He was, after all, past forty and at an age when a man needed a nap after a long ride and a heavy meal. She stood up and crossed to where he leaned back, chin sunk in the velvet of his doublet.

If you saw him like this, Nan Bullen, how would you feel? Would you ache with the desire to reach out and touch him, or do your fingers crave only the bright glitter of a crown? I endured his high and selfish youth, bore and buried his children, knew his moments of glory and despair. I have the right to share his middle years, to hold in my heart the quietness of his old age. And I am robbed of that, forced to protect myself and my child against the man whom I shall always love.

She had fought so hard. With the Bullen wench back at Court it had been misery, and an even greater misery to know that the girl was chaste. Playing at cards with the slant eyed lady-in-waiting, the Queen had even been forced into a grudging tribute.

'You have the good fortune to stop at a King, but I believe you will have all or nothing.'

All for Nan Bullen, it seemed; and for Queen Katherine only the humiliation of an appearance in Court where, kneeling before the unmoving and unmoved King, she had made her passionate plea.

'Sir, I beseech you, for the love that has been between us and for the love of God, let me have justice and right. I flee to you as to the head of justice within this realm. This twenty years I have been your true and lawful wife, and by me have you had many children. Although it pleased God to take them that was no fault in me. And I take God to be my judge that when you had me first I was a true maid without touch of man. And whether this be true or not I put it to your conscience.'

He had not answered nor looked at her. Only the voice of the Crier had followed her into the street.

'Katherine, Queen of England, come again into the Court! *Katherine, Queen of England, come into the Court!*'

She held the shirt up to her face, whispering, 'Oh, God, help us both.'

Mary's quiet step sounded as she returned with the pills in her hand, but she was hushed by a warning finger and came to stand by her mother.

'If we could only stay like this,' she whispered. 'If it were not for that woman!'

She said nothing more but there was hatred in her tight young face as if something shrivelled within her too soon.

THE TIME
OF THE WHITE FALCON

❈❈❈

CHAPTER FOUR

Anne had burst in among the courtiers as they rested in the orchard after the day's hunting. There had been in her beauty a new triumph, glittering, dangerous, half-hysterical, and her laughter had shrilled out as she called across to her poet-cousin.

'Have you an apple about you, my sweet Tom? I have an incredible fierce desire for an apple. The King says this means I am with child!'

With child, with child, with child!

It echoed round the land from council chamber to tavern. The goggle-eyed whore was swollen-bellied; the citadel of the lady had finally fallen before the onslaught of the King. At the precise moment when, almost without realising it, he wearied of the chase, the quarry had surrendered, and not death but a new life would follow. There would be a son for the King, an heir for England, and those about the throne must bestir themselves and make certain this child was born in wedlock.

The Cardinal had died, not of the plague but of a broken heart, it was said. Of fear, more likely, Anne's friends scoffed, for had not the butcher's cur been ordered to leave his retirement in York and journey to the Tower, there to answer charges of malpractice? Bishop Fisher was also in the Tower, having twittered too loudly and too often about his support for Queen Katherine. And Thomas More had resigned the Chancellorship, and watched the stars alone from the roof of his Chelsea home.

There were new men now about the King, and two of them were proving particularly useful. When Henry thought of Secretary Cromwell and of Archbishop Cranmer a gleam of satisfaction lit his eyes. What Cromwell lacked in finesse he made up in resolute energy, and what Cranmer lacked in forcefulness he redeemed by subtlety of intellect. Good servants both and devoted to their master, whose cause they made their own. Cromwell's appointment had been one of Henry's brighter inspirations, and Cranmer's rise to the See of Canterbury had been confirmed by Rome.

The two men made a strange contrast as they talked together in a small chamber at Westminster. The new Archbishop had a spare, stoop-shouldered frame and a mournful face set apologetically on a long neck. His companion was a shorter, chunkier individual with slant-lidded eyes and a square jaw.

As he talked he moved his shoulders in a restless, jerky fashion as if he craved action of some kind. Almost before Cranmer could insert a quiet greeting, he had launched upon a tirade against the lewd inscriptions scrawled on the walls of the city.

'Such things cast grave dishonour upon the King! They are treason, my lord, and must be stopped. And the only way to silence these slanders, to blot out these abominable libels, is to regularise the Lady Anne's position. Have you observed the street walls, my lord? The filth pictured on them?'

'You must give me time, Master Secretary.'

Cranmer spoke mildly, putting up his hands as if to ward off impending time, but Cromwell thrust forward his bull neck.

'Mistress Bullen is with child,' he persisted. 'There *is* no time. Five full years His Grace has waited on the Pope's decision and he is losing patience.'

'I think Rome must give ground now,' the Archbishop mused hopefully. 'We have mustered such a body of opinion from the Universities, it cannot fail to influence His Holiness.'

'Cranmer, there is only one opinion His Holiness can afford to entertain,' Cromwell said impatiently. 'The Emperor has him in his power and Charles will not see his aunt divorced. That is unalterable.'

'But we must have His Holiness' consent. Without it the future heir could be pronounced illegitimate,' Cranmer pointed out.

'Would you have His Grace answer the Papal summons and crawl to Rome on his knees?' Cromwell demanded.

'The people would never assent to it.'

'Precisely.' The secretary banged the clenched fist of one hand into the palm of the other. 'You want the Papal blessing on this divorce. It will not be granted. Therefore'—the heavy shoulders twitched—'we must divorce the Pope.'

Cranmer pulled at his chin, and looked doubtful.

'His Grace won't like that,' he ventured.

'He is halfway to it,' Cromwell asserted. 'Head of the Church of England. We have only to complete the separation. My lord Archbishop, it is our business, yours and mine, to clear the ground before His Grace, remove the stones, the filth, the rubbish, that might offend his royal eye. That's where my late master Wolsey failed and where I shall not fail. Because I anticipate the King's wishes. Now—does he want his new Queen full-bellied at her Coronation?'

He shot out the question as if he were spitting excrement, and Cranmer's features quivered slightly with distaste, but he answered mildly, with no more than a trace of self-satisfaction.

'I have already prepared the annulment of His Grace's union with the Lady Katherine and drawn up all necessary papers proclaiming her Princess Dowager. Within a day of this sentence the King's new marriage can be confirmed and the lady's coronation may then take place.'

So the sly fox knew that the King and the Concubine were already wed. Cromwell's broad face crinkled into a smile.

'I did not think to have under-estimated you,' he bowed. 'My dear Cranmer, what you needed was not time. It was reassurance.'

'Others will need that too.' Cranmer spoke sadly. 'The Lady Katherine and the Lady Mary—we must make matters as easy for them as we can. They are popular, you know. And it is important to gauge the temper of the mob.'

'Send up a few fireworks and fill the conduits with wine, and the mob will shout loudly for Queen Anne Boleyn,' Cromwell advised.

'No doubt. Crowds are fickle,' the Archbishop sighed.

'It is the King we serve, not the mob,' Cromwell reminded him. 'We wait upon His Grace according to our talents, our courage——'

'Or our cowardice.'

For some reason the calm, quiet faces of old Bishop Fisher and Thomas More hovered in his mind. This was their winter season, cast into the icy wastes of royal displeasure. For the Lady Anne it was high, wild summer, and there was a madness of desire in the air.

She rode to her Coronation in an open litter, her swelling stomach concealed under a robe of cloth-of-gold, her black hair flowing loose to the cushions on which she sat. The streets were scrubbed clean of their offensive murals, bordered now with banners and tableaux depicting her device of a crowned falcon, holding in its beak a blunt-petalled Tudor rose. The green-hosed archers threw their caps into the air, cheering for her, and the white-cassocked boys of the Chapel Choir spun melodies.

But she could not avoid noticing that the crowds

who packed the narrow streets, leaned from the windows and clung to the cornices, were, for the most part, silent. It mattered nothing, for the opinion of the mob was of small account. The people were sentimentalists, traditionalists, preferring an ageing, barren, foreign woman to a beautiful English lady who wore the King's ring upon her finger and carried the King's seed under her heart.

The papers announcing the birth of the prince had already been drawn up, the lying-in-chamber prepared, the name of Henry chosen. Now it was for Anne to play her part and bear a healthy, living son.

Watching from a window of the Palace as a carnival dragon spat fire into the evening sky, she felt the King's eyes upon her and turned, holding out her hand to him. In the window-panes the jewels of her crown—specially made so that it would rest lightly on her brow—danced and shimmered, their colours broken into a myriad rainbows.

Henry pressed his hand against her stomacher and the child leapt within her, reminding them both of the true reason for this marriage that had turned the kingdom upside down.

The baby was born under the sign of Virgo in the Chamber of the Virgins. Anne pointed out the fact in a weak, breathless voice, while her pain-sunken eyes searched the King's face anxiously as he bent over the gilded cradle.

'She is a bonny child,' he said at last. 'And she shall bear my late mother's name.'

'I wish it had been a—son.'

She clasped her hands together under the bedclothes, willing an amused smile to her lips.

'Sweetheart, we shall make a boy next time!' he said heartily.

She nodded, smiling as he lifted the child, pillowed on lace, to display her to the Court. Next time they would make a boy. *Next time!!!*

All the world ought to rejoice at the birth of a healthy child. The King certainly made merry, though some whispered he was merely putting a good face on it. The cheerfulness was not much in evidence however when he learned that the Pope, acting no doubt on the Emperor's instructions, had excommunicated him, or threatened to, unless he put away his new Queen, and took Katherine back into his bed.

Cranmer, listening to the King's roaring as they sat in Council, thought wryly that it was all very well for His Holiness to threaten from the safe distance of Rome. A poor Archbishop of Canterbury had to endure the backlash.

'Excommunicate me! Let him excommunicate me—I don't care two straws!' Henry said, snapping his fingers viciously and glaring round as if they were all Popes.

'He only threatens it, Your Grace,' Cranmer reminded him.

'Let him!' Henry retorted. 'Let him forbid me the Mass, deny me burial, cast me into hell fire—shall I now kiss his ring? I will give His Holiness such a buffet as he never had! His name shall be obliterated from all books of public worship and he shall be known in future by his correct title—the Bishop of Rome!'

From the foot of the table, the Duke of Norfolk, more grizzled and spare since the day when he had flung the Scots King's coat down before Henry, voiced the fears of the older nobility.

'Your Grace, are we not in danger of a divided kingdom, a two-headed monster?'

'Is your allegiance divided, Norfolk?' Henry rapped.

'No, Your Grace!'

'No more is my kingdom's.' Henry drew a deep breath. 'Obedience to the Pope,' he burst out, 'to the

Bishop of Rome, is unmanly, unholy—and un-English. From this time, the Church shall pay its annates to me and a tenth of its revenues. If there is disaffection in the monasteries, we will search it out. Have you appointed commissioners?'

He barked the question at Cromwell, who sat hunched over the table, his massive head sunk into the thick neck, his eyes cold and bright.

'I have, Your Grace,' he said promptly. 'They will enquire also into the general conditions of these churchmen. In many cases drastic reforms are needed.'

The King had relaxed slightly, but a scowl hovered on his face.

Cromwell, with the air of a man who deals with the next item on the agenda, said briskly, 'Sir, regarding the Lady Mary——'

'I hear she's ill,' Brandon, Duke of Suffolk, put in.

'A slight indisposition,' Cromwell told him.

'Worse than that, I believe. I hear her mother has been asking for her to affect a cure.'

Suffolk, widower of the King's younger sister, had a soft spot for Katherine and her daughter, though it had not prevented him from escorting Anne to her Coronation.

'A physician has been sent to the Lady Mary,' Henry said sharply, as mention of his elder daughter induced in him a sensation of guilt as irritating as it was illogical.

'Would Your Grace consider rescinding their separation?' Cranmer ventured.

Provided with a focus for his irritation, Henry turned upon his Archbishop savagely.

'Not until they agree to the illegality of the marriage. Now they would only conspire together and incite rebellion, perhaps cause us to be invaded. They *must* submit. They must agree to the Succession of the

Princess Elizabeth until such time as the Queen bears me a son.'

'The Lady Katherine cannot forget she is of the royal line of Spain,' Suffolk said.

'Both she and the Lady Mary are primarily subjects of His Grace,' Cromwell said.

'Exactly!' Henry nodded approval at his Secretary. 'And they will swear to my Supremacy like any other subject. Any man, woman, or child that refuses shall find me in dead earnest. I don't care who he is—Fisher, More—he shall be put under attainder. These people shall learn the truth of the old prophecy—that I should begin my reign as a lamb, and become more raging than a lion.'

He made an abrupt gesture of dismissal and swung away, to stare through the window into the courtyard beneath. The Queen was passing through, surrounded by her ladies and some of the younger gentlemen. She had regained her looks since Elizabeth's birth and sparkled in a mantle red as her lips.

Katherine had never used paint but Anne painted cleverly, shading her mouth with carmine, exaggerating the slant of her eyes with kohl. Even now it was hard to realise that this brilliant, glittering creature was his; that she had opened doors into his life and swept, laughing and leaping, in and out of his dreams.

The Council were leaving, bowing to the King's unresponsive back. Cromwell shuffled his papers, waiting for the summons to remain behind when the others had gone, but Henry motioned towards Norfolk instead.

The two men stood together for a few minutes in silence, the room emptying and quietening. The Queen and her attendants had passed and the courtyard was empty too, save for a guard blowing on numbed fingers.

'Your son is well?' Henry spoke abruptly.

'Very well, Your Grace.'

'He is the same age as the Lady Mary. Let us hope he will be more dutiful.'

'Lady Mary has been too much under her mother's influence.'

'She must learn to set aside childish loyalties for the sake of duty. I have learned to do that,' Henry brooded.

'We must all learn to do that,' Norfolk said.

'Aye! All of you, all of you! You must learn who is your master, to whom you owe allegiance!'

'There are some who will be obstinate, Your Grace.'

'Root them out, destroy them!' Henry tugged at the fringed girdle of his gown and said, in a sudden, more quiet tone, 'If you can, save Thomas More for me.'

'He may not permit himself to be saved,' Norfolk warned, 'but, as his friend, I will try.'

The King nodded. He felt tired, with sadness replacing anger, and a weariness at his heart. Deep within him he knew that More would never submit. He had always known it ever since the night they had star-gazed together from the roof of More's home.

What was it that he had said? *I will serve you, provided I can keep a good conscience*. And I, too, Henry mused, live according to my conscience. God revealed to me through a series of dead boys that my union with Katherine was an incestuous, illegal thing. The Pope knows it too, but for political reason he shuts his eyes and threatens me with excommunication!

Anger was rushing back now, and it was easier to cope with anger. He was, after all, the King to whom all subjects owed absolute obedience. Wolsey had taught him that, and failed at the end because he had not applied the same rule of obedience to himself. It was not that Henry wished to control men's private opinions, but from all his servants he had the right to command public loyalty and support. Those who could not reconcile the two must be prepared to pay the penalty.

He was appalled in the months that followed to learn how many were prepared to pay. An endless stream of people seemed to wend their way to Tyburn where the executioners waited with the ropes, knives, and smoking fires. Many of them were obstinate Carthusians, dragged on hurdles over the spine-shattering cobblestones. A lifetime in the service of God made some men blindly stubborn.

'A mark on a piece of paper, acknowledging my Supremacy as Head of the Church, and they could return to their cells in peace!' Henry raged.

It was, of course, a personal insult to himself that they should favour a Pope they had never seen to the King who held their very lives in his hands! And so steeped were they in their disloyal superstition that neither starvation, nor the rack, nor the disembowelling knife could turn them from their suicidal purpose.

Not that the traitors were all Papists! The announcement of the King's Supremacy had brought such heresies to light that Henry was shaken to his soul. Men seemed to imagine that because he was Head of the Church, the sacred beliefs of that Church were now altered. So, alongside the monks of the Charterhouse, on the bumpy road to Tyburn, went men who argued against infant baptism, denied the Real Presence, questioned the virginity of the Holy Mother.

It was better to retire for a time to Hampton Court, where peaches clustered against the walls and the Queen came down to the archery butts to applaud his skill. Every month he asked her hopefully if she thought she might be pregnant again, and every month she tossed her coiled black head, laughing deep in her throat.

'You must give me time, sir! You must give me more time!'

For two of Henry's oldest friends there was no more time. Bishop Fisher was nearly eighty and so frail that he had to be supported up the steps to the scaffold on Tower Hill.

Fisher had been the King's tutor, had been intimately connected with the educational schemes put forward by the Lady Margaret Beaufort, Henry's learned and formidable grandmother. In John Fisher goodness and learning had combined, but in the end he too had proved stubborn and disloyal and prated of conscience.

'I condemn no man for his conscience. His may save him, but mine must save me,' he had said.

A stubborn, prating old fool who had outlived his usefulness. He had learned, as lesser men everywhere were learning, that the King was supreme and must be obeyed.

Even Thomas More had been forced to learn that lesson in the end. The King had strained every nerve to save him, even sending Norfolk to the Tower itself to plead with his old friend. But it had been quite useless, for More had never discovered how to bend. He could only stand firm or be cut down, and his death must serve as a warning to those who could not compromise.

At the end he had calmly jested with the headsman, and combed his hair as if he were bound for a wedding feast.

Before laying his head upon the block he had declared, 'I die the King's good servant—but God's first.'

So he had not forgotten their conversation so long ago, and in the end he too had proved false to friendship. Yet his head, spiked on the central turret of London Bridge, reproached Henry's dreams.

CHAPTER FIVE

It was too warm to dance or to ride, even if the Queen's condition had permitted her to take such a risk. Instead, she sat within doors in the cool space of her apartment, her hands idle as she listened to her musician play. A handsome lad, Mark Smeaton, with insolent gypsy eyes. He caressed her with those eyes even as his brown fingers plucked the lute.

Her other friends lounged on cushions about her feet. It was, she thought idly, flattering to a lady's vanity that such personable gallants as Norris, Weston and Brereton should choose to spend their time with her. Jane Rochford sat a little apart from the rest, with her nose in the air. Trust Milady Rochford for that! Anne wondered how her brother could abide to be married to such a woman.

The King stood in the doorway, watching the group. Anne became aware of him gradually and her attention withdrew from the melody and focused upon her husband's black suit and close-cropped red head. She had never seen him look so despondent before.

As the tune died into silence he roused himself to say, with a creditable imitation of his usual heartiness, 'A fine air, Master Smeaton.'

The others had scrambled to their feet, bowing, as Lady Rochford insinuated herself into a curtsey.

'Will Your Grace favour us with one of his own?' Norris asked.

'Not now. I wish to speak to the Queen.'

He made a weary motion of dismissal and stood, eyes downcast, as they filed out.

'You have cut off your hair, sir.'

Anne went to him, her hand stretched out, but he made no move to clasp it.

'You look tired,' she coaxed. 'Come, rest.'

The great, canopied bed beckoned them, but he evaded her glance and moved away.

'Shall I read to you? I have marked some passages in the new books.'

She made her voice light, her face cheerful. Henry looked at her for a long moment, seeing beyond her features the spiked head on the bridge.

'The most honest man in my kingdom,' he said at last. 'You are the cause of his death, Madam; of all their deaths.'

If he had spoken violently it would have been less alarming, but the heaviness of his voice set her trembling.

'Sir, it was their own wilful disobedience. You had the courage to crush them, as you did Wolsey, and ensure peace for your realm.'

She smiled as she finished, leaning back amid the silken pillows, holding out her arms to him. He stumbled a little as he went towards her and then he was holding her very tightly, muttering in the sulky tone of a small boy.

'It has made a fearful noise throughout Europe.'

'If we listened to every slander, sir, we should soon be pease pudding!' Anne mocked. 'And you should be more audacious yet.'

'In what manner?'

'The Dowager Duchess and her child are still at large and could do you great harm,' she dared. 'Mistress Mary should be wed to some private gentleman.'

'My daughter?'

'Your bastard, sir,' she corrected swiftly. 'Marry her off, or let her be placed as maidservant to Elizabeth.'

But she had spoken too recklessly. He stiffened in her arms and there was a coldness in his voice.

'We will think on it.'

'But not now. Now you shall forget these cares. I have planned a feast for us, sir, a great revel. Even the Imperial Ambassador shall be invited——'

'Masques? Mummeries?' Henry's voice was eager again.

'And very curious disguisings—of the Ethiop Queen and her train.'

Henry raised himself on his elbow and looked down at her. When she smiled her teeth showed white and sharp, and her eyes were pure black with no trace of amber. Lust shook him like a wind and he put his hand to her throat, tugging at the jewelled band which hid the mole raised on the honeyed skin.

'Yes, you shall be the Ethiop Queen with your dark eyes, your sweet, slender—do not hide it.'

His voice thickened as he pushed away her restraining hand, and he buried his face into her neck, sucking and nibbling at the sweet, disfigured flesh.

'Why did you take my letters?' She pulled away slightly to ask. 'The ones you sent to me when I was at Hever? I had them tied together and locked most securely.'

'I don't have them, sweetheart. They'll come to light no doubt——'

He wondered vaguely what had brought the letters into her mind and then thought was drowned in a rising tide of desire, and her little moan of ecstasy was lost in the muffled drum-beat of his turbulent heart.

They returned to Greenwich in time for the reception for the Imperial Ambassador. Arrangements for the occasion were in the Queen's hands, and there was a great deal of smothered laughter behind closed doors and whisking of skirts around corners whenever the King appeared. It was to be a joyous occasion, designed to set a seal on the splendour of the year, to turn men's minds from rotting heads and the stench of burning entrails.

On this night only candles and rushlights were ablaze, and in the great hall of the palace ladies fluttered like moths near the leaping fires that cast a soft glow over painted features and jewelled coifs. It was a night for gaiety, for music, for whispering in corners, lips close to a lover's ear.

The King sat at the high table with Signor Chapuys at his side. Anne had borne them company during the main part of the meal but then had slipped away. She had been quiet, with a reckless little smile on her mouth such as she wore when she set her horse at a high jump or gambled her month's allowance on the turn of a card. Henry, noticing, felt an uneasiness in the pit of his stomach.

It had been something of a diplomatic triumph to persuade Chapuys to attend, and he hoped Anne would behave with the dignity due to her position. There were times when she would laugh shrilly in public or bend towards her attendants, joking with them as if they were her equals.

He fidgeted a trifle, casting a sidelong glance at the Ambassador. Before them, in the wide cleared space below the table, five couples danced to the beating of kettledrums and the occasional scream of a trumpet. The performers had darkened faces and hands, but Anne's white teeth gleamed through the make-up, and her feet wove intricate and sinuous patterns beneath her loose robe. Her hand was locked in the hand of her partner, and the King frowned slightly, recognising her musician.

In the corner, where a fluttering arras provided shelter and privacy of a sort, Weston and Norris lounged, goblets half-drained, and the excitement of pleasurable scandal on their faces.

'The Queen dances with Smeaton tonight.'

'And have you marked her intimacy with the music-man?'

'Groom of the Chamber soon. I heard it privately,' Norris murmured.

'From gypsy to Groom.' Weston let out a soundless whistle as his eyes followed the Queen, now swaying to and fro in Smeaton's grasp with her own eyes half-closed. Then she thrust him away with an imperious gesture and danced on alone, faster and faster to the whirling music while her female attendants circled her slowly.

Henry cleared his throat and spoke uncomfortably. 'You admire the masque, Signor Chapuys?'

'Most elegant, sir, especially Her Grace's steps.'

It was impossible to tell if the Ambassador was hiding a faintly contemptuous smile.

'All her own devising,' Henry said. 'She has a great love of music.'

'As I have heard.'

Chapuys was quite definitely smiling now. The King's glance shifted to the dancers again and the vein in his forehead swelled slightly as the music rose to a deafening climax. The dancers spread fanlike around the glittering, darkened Queen who stood for an instant poised on the edge of movement and then, snatching a riding whip from a kneeling attendant, cracked it three times through the feverish air.

Now Smeaton returned, leading a portly figure dressed in the scarlet robes of a Cardinal, and the music began again as a mocking echo to the dancers who circled the figure of parody, pointing and twisting until it crumpled to its knees before the Queen. And she, sweat shining through the darkness of her face, took a scimitar and waved it in phantom execution over the sagging head.

'By God—it's meant to be Wolsey!'

Norfolk's horrified growl was lost in a final clash of

cymbals as the Queen advanced to the table and curtsied low to the King.

There was applause, louder in some quarters than others, and a wary buzz of conversation. The Queen's voice was pitched a shade too high and her breasts heaved.

'Your Queen salutes you, O Solomon.'

But his Queen was plump and fair and sat in gentle dignity while her lord threw a golden trophy into her lap.

'You are dark, Madam,' he said.

'Scorched by the hot sun, sir!'

As others would never, could never be again. Fisher, More, Wolsey himself who had taught the King how to be a King—hounded into their graves and mocked as they lay in them!

'You know my meaning,' he grated. 'Wanton. Extravagant, Madam, to treat a cardinal in such a fashion.'

'I am Queen of a wild land, sir,' she answered defiantly, 'and I may do as I please in it.'

The King's eyes were narrow and his breath came short.

'Take care, Madam,' he rasped, and the throbbing temple vein, the white line about his mouth spoke a message even she could understand.

'It was but a masque, sir, like any other——' she began, but he cut her short.

'I think not. It lacked respect.'

'Sir, you have often blacked your face and wielded a sword in dumb show——'

'That will do. No more.'

His voice cut through her stumbling words and she stared at him, her mouth a little open, displaying the sharp white teeth. The spectators had broken up into groups, each group laughing and chattering as if a silence would be fatal.

Henry pushed aside his chair and stepped from the daïs, turning from the Queen and striding down the hall. He was aware of nothing at that moment but a blind and choking rage. He had not realised her capable of such petty, ill-bred malice. Her antics had cheapened him before the whole Court. And everywhere he looked he saw the darkened faces of her attendants, as if they all wore one mask and that the mask of malice.

The girl stood alone with her back to the tapestry, and some quality of stillness in her held his attention. Her face was innocent of paint and glimmered greenish-white against the dark arras. There was something fresh and springlike about her and as she sank into a curtsey a faint scent of lavender rose to his nostrils.

'Mistress—Seymour, is it not?'

He made an effort to speak gently, for she was trembling slightly and her eyes flickered nervously to where Anne stood with Signor Chapuys at her side.

'Your Grace.'

She began to sink into a second curtsey, but he put out his hand.

'Get up, get up,' he said. 'I have seen you before—at Court?'

'Sir, I was maid-in-waiting to Queen Ka—— to the Princess Dowager.'

She flushed and twisted her fingers together, her coifed head drooping.

She was older then than he had imagined, nearer thirty than twenty, but there was an unawakened air about her.

'We are pleased to see you returned, Mistress Seymour,' he said soothingly, and saw her blush again, the blood racing under her white skin.

At the other side of the room, Chapuys was saying politely to an unheeding Queen, 'I admired your ballet, Madam. And I understand from the King that Your Highness is to be blessed with another child in the New Year.'

He stopped, his eyes following her gaze to where Henry talked with the pale young woman. There was nothing comical in the pair but Anne, watching them, burst out laughing suddenly.

'Have I said something to amuse Your Grace?' the Ambassador ventured.

'Forgive me, sir.' Her husky voice shook with mirth and there were tears in her eyes.

She wanted to explain that she laughed because—but she didn't know the reason. She only knew that she had to go on laughing, as those nearest to her ceased their own talk and turned to stare at her. Norris had come to her and was offering wine—red wine in a ruby goblet. Henry was still talking to Mistress Seymour, bending low as if to shield her. For no reason at all, Anne thought of Katherine. The Spanish wife would smile to witness this little comedy. Anne herself could not restrain her own shrill peals.

But the Spanish wife was past all mirth. In the bitter January, Chapuys knelt at the bedside of the one they now called Princess Dowager and kissed the dropsy-swollen hand. Kimbolton was not the most cheerful of residences even for a woman in good health. For a dying one, the small, ill-lit chamber, with the foul rushes beating themselves against the stone in the draught from the ill-fitting door, must have been torture.

And Katherine *was* dying. He had seen that waxy, pinched look over the nostrils before. Her voice still held its dignity however and there was a trace of lingering sweetness in her smile.

'Signor Chapuys, we thank you for the courtesy of this visit.'

'Madam, the King, the whole country are most gravely concerned for your health,' he told her.

'Yes, they bring me fruit. Apples and—delicacies.' She coughed, and seeing his eyes on the sparse furniture and threadbare hangings said, 'Your Excellency must forgive us, we are not well appointed here.'

'When you are recovered, Madam,' Chapuys said swiftly, 'the King has promised that you shall be moved to a warmer residence.'

'Has he?' She gave the two words a little, ironic inflection that showed she was not deceived.

'And that all arrears of your pension shall be paid in full,' he plunged recklessly on.

'Signor——' she whispered and motioned him to lean closer. 'I thank God that you and my good friend, Maria, have come.'

She gestured affectionately towards Maria de Salinas who stood, face averted, a little distance away.

'She travelled her alone,' Katherine said proudly. 'She forced them to admit her and she has been with me ever since. Now I shall not die like one of the beasts.'

'You must give yourself every chance, Madam,' he urged. 'The peace and unity of Christendom depend on your life.'

'I was thinking of Mary,' she said, as if Christendom had lost its meaning and the world had shrunk to dear, familiar things. 'Have you seen my daughter, sir?'

'Yes, Madam.' Chapuys thought of the slim, fair-haired girl who had been so merry as a child and was now so grave and silent. 'She is in better health.'

'Does she eat more? She was not eating well.'

'She is eating more, Madam. Yes, indeed,' he reassured.

'But he will not let her come to me?' Katherine murmured.

He knew what it must cost her to ask the question, for so long as it remained unanswered she could allow herself a last, faint delusion of hope. Chapuys wished that he could utter a comforting lie, but some trustful quality in the sunken eyes stilled his tongue.

Maria de Salinas cried out in sudden anguished violence, *'Es la maldita mujer Ana Bolena! La Puta!'*

'Hush, Maria.' Katherine's voice strengthened into reproof. 'You should pray for her.'

'You are too generous, Madam,' Maria choked. 'To her and to the King!'

'He is not ill-natured in himself,' Katherine excused. 'He has been much troubled.'

And I, her mind accused, was his greatest trouble, for I could not bear him a living son. But it was God's Will, not God's punishment upon our union. I had to do what my conscience told me was right. If there had been no child at all—but there was Mary. I could not let them name her bastard.

Her lips twitched wryly, for they had done it anyway, and now Mary was kept away from Court, forbidden to see her own mother; and Katherine herself lay in what was little better than a prison.

And who am I to complain when the poor monks who still upheld my title were racked almost asunder before their executions? And the great men who were my friends and the King's friends—Fisher, Thomas More.

'Signor, I only wanted the good of England,' she said fretfully, 'and I have brought it little good.'

'Madam, you could have done no more than you did,' Chapuys soothed, but she turned her head restlessly from side to side.

'When I was wed to Prince Arthur they did not send all my dowry at once and it was a great shame to me,' she said. 'And later, after I married the King, my father made a separate peace with France. Henry was angry, justly angry.'

'Madam, you must rest now.'

The Ambassador had interpreted a warning shake of the head from Maria.

'Rest? Yes, I will rest. But first I will sign the letter which you shall take to the King.'

Katherine raised herself painfully on the cushions and gestured to the table against the wall.

Maria, her olive face stony, brought the little travelling desk, the sheet of writing, the pen, and stood back again as Katherine's hand moved slowly, tracing her name. Her lips shaped the words aloud with a dogged, patient obstinacy.

'Katherine, Queen of England.'

It was, thought Chapuys, as he knelt to kiss her hand and receive the sealed message, a comment on her own existence. Not for one single moment would she abandon her principles or consent to be named as less than she was.

Had she been more pliable or more beautiful—but then she would not have been Katherine. Mingled with the Ambassador's deep admiration was a spasm of irritation at the woman who would permit a whole nation to be torn apart rather than give up her own rights.

'The physicians say that she is sinking fast,' Maria told him as she escorted him down the stairs to the main hall. 'It is a great miracle that she has lasted so long. Hurried from one damp dwelling to another, deprived of warm clothing and fresh air, fearful lest her food be poisoned!'

'The Queen has great courage,' he allowed.

'She is a saint,' Maria said fiercely. 'That letter you hold in your hand. She gave it to me to read. Do you know what she says in it to the King—to *him*? She says, "Above all things mine eyes desire to see you."'

'She loves him still,' Chapuys said.

'With all her heart! Is that not a strange thing, signor.'

The Ambassador smiled a little and thought that the ways of women were always strange.

❉❉ CHAPTER SIX ❉❉

The King had decided that the ways of women frustrated all human understanding. It was surely natural to grieve a little for one's brother's widow, and no more than was due a Princess Dowager to order Court mourning at her death. Jane, little sweet Jane, had gone at once into black and her eyes had been red-rimmed, for she had been maid-in-waiting to Katherine.

Anne had worn yellow and dressed her attendants in the same tactless shade. It was worse than tactless! It bore the same element of mockery, of lack of breeding, that she had displayed in the masque when she had insulted a dead Cardinal. Of course she was very near her time, and women often took odd notions into their heads when they were great with child. But in Anne's case spells of almost hysterical gaiety alternated with fits of screaming temper.

She was in a rage now, screeching like a fishwife, as she followed Henry into her chamber.

'If I am Queen, and now that I truly am, I demand that you send Mistress Seymour from this Court!'

'Demand, Madam?' He broke in harshly, reddish brows lifted. 'In all the years I lived with Katherine there was no demanding. You assume privileges that are not yours.'

'And you make presents to that pallid little mouse!'

'Nonsense,' he said uneasily, but she swung round, glaring at him.

'A locket? A sapphire locket with your image in it?'

'Ha!'

He made an abrupt dismissing noise, but she opened her clenched fist, showing the trinket.

'Then what is this,' she shrieked, 'that I found about Mistress Seymour's *neck*?'

For an instant her hands twisted as if Jane's neck were between them. Then she flung the locket past Henry with such violence that it splintered against the wall.

He had fastened the chain about Jane's throat with his own hands, seeing the delicate veins throb under the unblemished skin. Before, she had worn only a simple gold cross, for though her brothers were coming men, Jane had been reared in country fashion, and was unsophisticated. And now, the Queen had torn away the friendly little gift and broken it, just as she spoiled everything in his life that was clean and sweet.

'By God, you——!' he bellowed, and saw fear in her slanted eyes; saw too the gross, distended belly that sheltered England's heir. For the sake of the child he dared not lose his temper. Instead he tried to soothe her, though a red mist hung still before his eyes.

'You are upset now and need rest. You must take care of our child. The physicians predict it will be a son, Madam—a fine son—they all say it, the astrologers, the cunning women. Now be at peace, sweetheart, and all shall go well with you. Rest.'

He patted her shoulder awkwardly.

'While you go to that Seymour wench!' she blazed at him.

'No, Madam, but to exercise.'

Henry felt such a desire to escape from her that he said the first thing that came into his head, and almost ran from her shrill weeping. But the idea was attractive. It was a fine, cold day with a sharp rime upon the ground. A man could not be expected to sit indoors for ever, waiting for a child to be born. And he had put on far too much weight recently. Jane was so slim and small.

Mounted on his chestnut gelding, with the wind stinging the tips of his ears and his companions streaming behind him, the King was himself again. The glamour of the hunt lay in the excitement of the chase, for often the quarry was worth little in the end.

The stag had been sighted. Norfolk gave a high, clear yell of delight and they spurred through the thick woodland towards the open meadows, fanning out as they thundered down the grassy slope. Sheep scattered, bleating, and a flock of small birds gossipped indignantly as they flew to a safer distance.

Ahead of the riders, a stone wall, built to mark some division of property, rose up. Suffolk and the others were veering right, but the King set his chestnut at the wall. Not for a monarch the cautious detour!

The stones, rough-veined, sharp edged, blocked the horizon. The horse gathered itself for the jump and rose too soon. The wall, the sky, the ground, tumbled together into blackness.

He was aware of an aching head and a dry mouth, and a fierce, bone-grinding pain from hip to ankle. Anxious faces bent over him, and then he slipped back into unconsciousness again.

He woke to pain and poulticing and blood-letting and such a disorganised atmosphere of gloom that he began to fear the accident had hurt him worse than he knew. It was Cranmer of the sad eyes and pouched cheeks who told him at last that the Queen had given birth to a dead son.

The pain was not in his leg now, but in his heart, concentrated there like some evil thing which devoured all other feelings. This was the son for whom he had longed all his life. This was England's heir, conceived to continue a dynasty and rule a nation. For this boy he had put aside a loyal and faithful woman, banished his daughter, executed his friends—and

Anne had borne a dead babe. First another daughter, for which he had forgiven her, and now this.

Anger drove out pain; not hot, bubbling temper which quickly cooled, but an icy rage which seared, building scar tissue over a wounded nature.

He had himself wheeled to her bedside and looked with sick loathing at the sharp face and the thin, flat shape under the quilts. She had almost died, the physicians told him, and he wished savagely that she had died and freed him of her presence.

It was as if the blow on the head had knocked the scales from his eyes and he saw everything as it really was; saw clearly that Anne was past thirty and had begun to lose her looks, that her gaiety and charm sprang not from the warmth of an affectionate heart but from a lust to dominate and possess.

She had dared to make some feeble excuses, to weep a little, but he was past believing in her pain or her repentance. And it angered him further to see the courtiers flock about her door—Weston, Brereton, Norris, her brother George, and that insolent gypsy who disturbed a sick room with his discords.

To Cromwell he cried furiously, 'What remedy? Find me a remedy!'

His minister's heavy jowls quivered slightly and a thoughtful look came into the flat-nosed face. Cromwell said nothing but his bow promised action.

King and Queen enjoyed a separate convalescence. Anne recovered quickly and was heard laughing and joking with her friends, as if, thought Henry, she bore no guilt for the loss of the child.

He complained about it bitterly to Jane when he visited her in her apartment. It pleased him to sit, his bandaged foot propped on a stool, and watch Jane as she listened, her fair head bent and her small hands folded quietly.

Katherine had always sewed when he was with her.

The rasp of silk being drawn through silk had irritated his nerves. Anne seldom allowed him to finish a sentence without interrupting. Jane sat still, attending to his words.

'It was your fall, sir,' she said, excusingly. 'I was there when the Duke came to tell us of it. Shortly afterwards the Queen took to her bed. We were afraid you would not live.'

'It was the child who died,' he reminded her. 'And it is now too sure that God will give me no sons by her.'

There was trouble in her face. She looked up and her voice trembled.

'Your Grace, let me leave Greenwich. I cannot disobey your command but if I were gone, sir, you and Her Grace——'

'No. I will have no more issue by her,' he interrupted, and leaned across, imprisoning Jane's hands between his own as words poured out of him. 'Jane, I have been as a blind man these ten years. Everything my people ever said of her is proved right. I was seduced into this marriage—by witchcraft. In Christ's name, she even has the marks upon her—upon her neck, upon her finger. She tries to hide them but they are the devil's stigma.'

'Sir,' she gasped, awkwardly, 'I can say nothing of this.'

'You will have seen them surely? The mole upon the neck? The extra finger?'

As he stood up, reaching wincingly for his stick, Jane moved away, her placidity gone and tears wetting her lashes.

'I only know that she bears you a great love, sir, and that my presence here may have caused her to miscarry,' Jane said wretchedly. 'Your Grace must let me go now, before I harm her further—or my soul before God. I beg you, sir.'

That Jane should feel guilt when she had done nothing! It tore his heart.

'Let me leave Court for a while and return to Wiltshire, to my family.'

'Very well. You have our leave to go back to Wiltshire,' he said after a moment.

With Anne in her present mood she might try to harm Jane. It was best that such a gentle lady be removed for her own protection. He had a horrifying picture in his mind of a falcon ripping the petals from a snowdrop.

But when Jane had gone his life seemed meaningless again. If he could have banished Anne to some convent—but she was not past childbearing. At least ten years must pass before she was pronounced barren. If he had to spend ten years bound to the enchantress whose magic had failed, he would lose his mind.

He tried to avoid her as much as possible, but in public they still appeared together. And once, in an unguarded moment, he stepped out on to a balcony to take a breath of air and saw her below in the courtyard. She was setting two of her dogs to fight each other and as she crouched there, her teeth bared, she looked animal-like herself.

Henry must have made some sound for she glanced up, and the excited glitter in her eyes faded into a wary dullness. He stared at her for a moment and then moved away, the furious barking of the dogs echoing from the stone yard.

Almost three months since the death of the child, a full month since Jane had returned to her family!

'What remedy!' he cried again, to Cromwell.

'Mark Smeaton dines at my house tonight,' Cromwell said obliquely, and something in his expression stilled the King's queries.

It was the next morning that the questions were answered. Cromwell, his eyes slits of satisfaction, padded into the King's chamber and bowed with an air of having great information to impart.

'What is it?' Henry, who had been regretting his own ability to take part in the May Day contests, spoke sharply.

'This paper, Your Grace.' Cromwell held it out. 'It would repay your study of it.'

'Cannot we defer business until after——!'

Henry's eye fell upon the Queen's name and he began to read. The words were hammer-blows in his bewildered brain and the parchment rustled between his shaking hands. When he spoke, however, his voice was almost steady.

'How was this obtained?'

'Why, Smeaton confessed to me personally, sir.' Cromwell nodded sadly. 'He admits to three separate violations.'

'And the others? Those he implicates?'

'Brereton on November the sixteenth, Norris on the nineteenth——' Cromwell began to tick them off on spatulate fingers.

'Good God,' Henry said in a low voice. 'Dear God.'

'I fear to continue,' Cromwell hesitated, 'lest I anger Your Grace.'

Henry tapped the document in a parody of his normal manner.

'Do you believe this, Cromwell?' he whispered.

'Sir, I am forced to when I consider the evidence,' Cromwell said reluctantly. 'And the expenses outlaid by Master Smeaton—where did he get so much money if not from the Queen?'

Smeaton had worn a yellow doublet on the day that Katherine was buried. Anne's eyes had rested upon him as he knelt before her.

And the others—Norris, Brereton, even her own—Henry's mind censored the word. Had they too known the thin-hipped, small-breasted body, heard the moan of anguished delight?

'Your Grace was to attend the May Day lists,' Cromwell was saying. 'I believe you should still attend them, sir.'

Henry nodded slowly. For his own peace of mind he would have to see the Queen, watch her closely, satisfy himself as to her innocence or guilt.

But it was not easy to stride down to the great tiltyard and take his place beside the Queen. It was not easy to school his expression to indifference when Anne gave him a brief inclination of her head and turned back immediately to chatter with Brereton.

The arena was gay with flags and banners, and great swathes of May-blossom, white petals curling in the bright sunshine. He fancied that the crowds cheered his arrival with more than usual warmth, but then they knew the Queen; perhaps they even dared to pity him as a cuckold King.

He dug his nails into the palms of his hands as Anne leaned forward, fluttering her lace handkerchief as a signal for the tilt to begin. Francis Weston was to ride first. The most beautiful man at Court, tittered the ladies. Beautiful as an angel, or a stallion. And Anne, thighs apart under the thin silk of her dress, lips parted, leaned forward to cry aloud in disappointment as Weston failed to break his lance.

'Let us hope Harry Norris can do better than that!' she exclaimed.

Brereton made some remark that Henry didn't quite catch. Anne inclined her ear towards him and then smiled at Henry. White, sharp teeth. Eyes tilted at the corners. What *had* Brereton said? 'Fling a smile in the King's direction lest he begin to suspect?' Why didn't she mention Smeaton's absence? Wouldn't it be the most natural thing in the world for her to remark that her musician had not yet returned from Cromwell's house?

Trumpets sounded again and Anne wiped perspiration from her brow with the scrap of lace. Henry turned his attention from her with an effort and frowned down the lists towards the barrier where Norris, visor down and lance uncouched, waited.

Again came the fluttering handkerchief. The rudimentary nail on her left hand grew under his eyes into a claw, stretching out to rip and tear. The joust began, and now, sharp-breasted, she leaned forward again. He could smell the excitement of her loins.

Harry Norris's lance splintered and the crowd rose, cheering. The Queen had risen too and was laughing, her throat quivering under its ribbon band.

Her handkerchief had fallen to the ground and lay, white and lacy, near to the horse on which the triumphant Norris sat, pushing back the visor to reveal his sweating face.

He had noticed the handkerchief, or perhaps the Queen had made some secret, private gesture. Henry couldn't tell, for the red mist was before his eyes again. Through the mist he saw Norris pick up the handkerchief on the shattered tip of his spear and mop the sweat from his own face. Sweat mingling, bodies writhing together, limbs naked and glistening in the aftermath of lust. The Queen was bending over the edge of the stand, her hand outstretched to receive back the handkerchief.

The King rose and pushed his way out, knocking aside a chair as he went, aware of the startled faces turned towards him, of the buzz of conversation that followed his precipitate departure.

At the back of the stand Cromwell waited to carry out his master's commands. Henry gave them in a cold, decisive manner.

'You will arrest Norris, Weston, Brereton and my lord Rochford immediately. Take the Queen later.'

Take Nan Bullen, the goggle-eyed whore who has

cheated me and cuckolded me, lending her body for a gypsy's pleasure, for her own brother's incestuous caress. Take Anne, my white falcon, who soared up into the air and flew too near to the sun, and fell, scorched and screaming, to the earth again.

Her own uncle, Norfolk, had taken her prisoner as she walked in her private orchard under the white May-blossom. They had rowed her to the Tower in the royal barge and the crowds had silently watched her pass.

They stood silently again, three weeks later, waiting in their hundreds. Silence had fallen too upon Westminster Palace as if the place lay under some evil spell, so that the ladies trod gently, shivering at shadows.

In the trees bordering the courtyard birds sang high in the green boughs as if they had escaped the magician's wand and knew only a careless animal rapture that took no account of human misery.

'So much singing,' Henry said, restlessly staring. 'Why is that?'

'I cannot think, Your Grace.'

It was Cranmer who answered. He had sent the others, even Cromwell, away, but his Archbishop was the one person whose company he could endure. Cranmer had visited Anne in the Tower, reporting that her outbursts of hysteria had given place to a bright and brittle gaiety. She had told Cranmer that the executioner's task would be easy, for she had but a little neck. By now it should have been severed but there had been a delay while a swordsman was brought from Calais. A sword was swifter and more efficient than the axe. And by now, surely, the deed would be done.

'I said noon. Is it past that yet?'

'No, Your Grace.'

The song of birds mocked him. Henry turned away from the window and came further into the room, his expression a blend of defiance and doubt.

'She is guilty, Cranmer,' he flung out.

'Two grand juries and twenty-seven peers found her so, Your Grace,' Cranmer agreed.

'But why? Why?' the King demanded. 'Why did she hold me off for so long and then—with those men? Her own brother even.'

It had horrified him more than anything else, that Anne and George Rochford could have bedded together. Rochford's wife had given evidence against her husband.

'Was it to get a son?' Henry asked. 'She laughed at me, you know, Cranmer—behind my back—boasting of my impotence.'

That at least was false, for he knew himself to be as virile as any man, but there were times when even a monarch grew weary. And Anne had sucked him dry.

'She conspired to poison the Lady Mary,' he said. 'And Katherine——'

Poor Katherine had died very suddenly at the end, a few weeks before Anne's child was due. Was there not cause for suspicion in that? There had been talk of poison then and the autopsy had revealed Katherine's heart to be black and rotten at the core: but that was wrong, for it was Anne who was evil. How could he even be certain that the dead baby had been his own son?

'Sir, I am sorry such faults were proven against the Queen,' Cranmer was saying. 'I never had a better opinion of woman. But I think Your Grace would not have gone so far if she had not been culpable.'

'She was in conspiracy to be rid of me,' Henry said.

'Then she has deserved her sentence,' Cranmer said quietly.

But I have not deserved mine, Henry thought. Anne will be dead, but I must live on in the knowledge of her guilt—if she *is* guilty. There came the question again, as memory with cruel caprice selected pictures for his torment.

Anne, at Hever, her hair about her shoulders and her arms raised to clasp his neck. Then, long lashes veiling her eyes, darting away, and the whisper in that husky voice.

'This is wrong, Sire, for you have a wife already.'

Anne, at Court, leaping higher than the other dancers, with her skirts spread wide and a diamond glinting in the shallow cleft between her breasts.

Anne, bow to her shoulder, taking careful aim at a buck and rippling with delighted laughter as the arrow found its mark.

Henry closed his eyes, but, behind the closed lids, Anne smiled on—at Rochford, at Weston, at Norris, at Brereton, at the damned gypsy!

Smeaton had called out to the watching crowd just before he was hanged, 'Masters, pray for me, for I have deserved the death!'

Deserved the death because he had been the Queen's lover? Or because he had lied, under torture at Cromwell's house? Guilty or innocent, black or white?

'So much singing,' Henry said. 'I shall ride out afterwards. I cannot remain here. I shall ride into Wiltshire.'

In Wiltshire there grew the snowdrop he longed to pluck. In Wiltshire there were meadows and hedgerows and a girl with blue eyes and little, gentle hands.

Cranmer gazed at him steadily, measuring the trend of his thoughts. In this ability lay much of the Archbishop's strength.

'May I remind Your Grace of the rogation days that lie ahead?' he ventured.

'Rogation?'

'If Your Grace intends to follow the advice of his Council, for the welfare of his realm, then your betrothal should be announced at once, sir,' Cranmer said.

The Archbishop was right, of course. It was a King's duty to marry again and beget a male heir for the Succession.

'Yes, see to it, my lord,' Henry nodded. 'I rely on your discretion.'

'Only that no marriage could be conducted on Ro——' Cranmer began, when the single boom from a cannon downriver startled the birds into the air.

The Archbishop knelt, his hands folded in prayer, and after a moment, the King knelt too. The remedy which he had demanded had been applied, but its bitterness would stay with him always now.

THE TIME OF THE SNOWDROP

❈❈❈

CHAPTER SEVEN

It had been a simple, family ceremony, quite different from the lush pageantry of his marriage to Katherine, the secrecy of the vows he had exchanged with Anne. Both false affairs, for Katherine had been his brother's widow and Anne had seduced him into marriage through witchcraft.

Jane Seymour was his first bride, and his last. He could only marvel that he had found her while he was still in the full virility of his manhood. Of course his leg pained him, having developed an ulcer which refused to heal, but for a man of forty-five he was in excellent health.

He wished Jane were more robust. Despite her country upbringing she was as slight as a child and very pale. Her two younger brothers towered over her. Henry liked both Edward and Thomas Seymour. Of the two, Edward had the more sense and ability, but there was about Thomas a devil-may-care charm that attracted the King.

Henry glanced back to where the young men paced together, a few tactful yards behind himself and his bride. With them came his favourite page, young Tom Culpepper.

They had all taken advantage of the warm summer afternoon to walk out from Wolf Hall through the flower-starred meadow. Jane stooped now and then to pick clover and limp-stemmed daisies, and weave them into a garland.

'When I was a child,' she confided to Henry, 'we used to make these wreaths on Lady Day and hang them on the statue of the Holy Virgin. And when evening came the boys used to take the garlands—each choosing his own small sweetheart's flowers.'

'And did they fight over your wreath?' Henry prepared to be jealous.

'Alas, no!' she answered gaily. 'My wreath was always left hanging there. I was not a pretty child, but my mother comforted me by saying I had great skill at making preserves!'

'You shall make some for me, after your Coronation,' Henry began, but she caught at his arm and her small face was troubled.

'Sire, I would not wish it,' she said earnestly.

'Not wish to be crowned? But you are the Queen,' Henry said.

'I am your wife. Nothing more and nothing less than your wife,' Jane insisted. 'For me there is no higher honour.'

'Modest Jane,' he teased, but something in him gloried at her meekness. It crossed his mind that she might have made a good nun but, when he said as much, Jane blushed and told him that she had always hoped to be married one day.

'I used to envy the village women with their babies,' she confided. 'Even peasants love their children and want the best for them.'

'Did your parents allow you to wander about?' Henry looked faintly shocked.

'Only if one of my brothers or a groom were with me,' she assured him. 'But I went often to the village.'

'Down that lane?'

He nodded towards a nearby track that skirted the meadow. From some little distance a group of poorly-clad people could be seen moving along it, and the sound of a rough chant could be heard.

'No, sir. That is the road to Hailes,' Jane explained. 'To the Abbey.'

'Have you been there?'

'Many times, sir.' Her eyes glowed at the recollection.

'And seen the Holy Phial, the Blood of Christ?'

'Yes, sir.'

She had bowed her head at the mention of the Holy name and he was struck afresh by her unselfconscious piety.

Following the King and glancing with a shadow of disapproval towards the chanting villagers, Edward Seymour remarked, 'They are crowding to Hailes now, since it was visited by the Commission.'

'The King's men are only anxious to report abuses,' Culpepper said in a mitigating tone.

'And to lay their hands on some of the gold ornaments,' Thomas Seymour remarked.

Culpepper cast a nervous glance ahead to where the royal couple walked.

'Your brother should guard his tongue, sir,' he muttered anxiously. 'It's safe with me, but not before His Grace.'

Edward nodded in his grave, considering way with the look on his face that made his resemblance to his sister most marked. Thomas, who seemed to have all the vigour that they lacked, clapped the page upon the shoulder.

'My thanks for the good advice, but His Grace appears more in need of your help at the moment.'

The King had indeed sat down wincingly on the lower step of a stile that marked the edge of the meadow.

'Shall I help you, sir?' Jane spoke anxiously as the others hurried up.

'No, no; some humour fallen into my leg. It's of no account.'

He spoke cheerfully but his face was grey with pain and he made no protest when Culpepper offered the support of his strong young shoulder.

It was evil mischance that his honeymoon should end with the breaking open of his ulcer, for with the end of honeymoon came a return to the cares of state that pursued him even in the peace of Hampton Court. By day he wrestled with problems in Council and by night he lay in an agony of wakefulness, his leg throbbing as if liquid fire shot along the nerves.

As dawn pearled the sky after one such night, the King struggled out of the great bed where Jane slept peacefully and lowered himself into a chair, easing his foot up to a stool. Through the window, in the increasing light, he could see a small group of musicians. Their tune drifted up to him and Jane stirred in her sleep, throwing out a slender arm towards the rumpled space beside her.

He spoke swiftly lest she should sleep again.

'I cannot rest. This throbbing will not let me rest.'

She was awake at once, pushing back the covers and reaching out for her robe.

'Let me call the physician, sir,' she said coaxingly, but he shook his head.

'He can do no good,' he said irritably. 'Nothing helps.'

'Shall I bid them stop their music?' she enquired.

'It pleases me,' he demurred. 'Signor Chapuys sends them to woo me on the Lady Mary's behalf.'

Jane had knelt by him and, with her long fair plaits, looked like a little girl about to ask a favour. He pulled one of the plaits teasingly.

'What ails you now?' he enquired.

'The Lady Mary was a friend of mine,' she hesitated. 'We are much of an age, sir, and we share many interests in common. Could Your Grace not find it in his heart to forgive her and to bring her and the little girl back from Hunsdon?'

Henry chose to ignore the reference to Elizabeth and said instead, in a tone of surprised displeasure,

'Bring Mary to Court?'

'Yes, sir.'

He bit his lip, frowning as he thought of Katherine's child. She was, of course, his child too and he had loved her and been proud of her until she had disobeyed him and sided with her mother.

'She's an unnatural girl,' he said at last.

'But you need her, sir, as she does you,' Jane pleaded. 'Young girls are often rebellious and it cannot have been easy for her, torn between two loyalties.'

'Jane, Jane, you are a fool,' he told her, and his voice was gentle. 'But kind. The kindest soul I ever met. You ought to seek the advancement of the children we will have, not any others.'

'The Lady Mary——' Jane began, but he pulled her down beside him.

'The Lady Mary is the most obstinate child that ever was,' he said in a tone that ended the discussion.

The most obstinate Lady Mary sat in the summer parlour at Hunsdon a month later and looked, with hollow, defiant eyes, across the small table at Signor Chapuys. He, cloaked and spurred, for he expected to have to leave as secretly as he had arrived, hid the pity in his face as he studied the haggard countenance before him.

The Lady Mary had lost her bloom. Grey already streaked the soft, fair hair and her mouth was pulled into a rigid and wary line. One cheek was swollen, for she had been enduring one of her frequent attacks of toothache, and her hands trembled as she pushed away the document she had been reading.

When she spoke, however, her voice was harshly decisive.

'I will not sign this thing!'

'Your Highness must do so.' The Ambassador was as firm as she was.

Tears quivered on her lashes.

'Signor Chapuys,' she said, shakily, '*you* ask this of me? The one friend I count on?'

'Madam, you have other friends,' he soothed. 'The Queen; Cromwell; the Archbishop——'

'Yes, you all advise me—and my Lord of Norfolk tells me that if I were his daughter he'd knock my head against the wall till it was baked apple! If I am put to any more——'

For a moment she bore an alarming resemblance to her father in one of his paroxysms of rage, and then she dropped her head in her hands.

'Madam,' Chapuys said firmly, 'I can no longer be responsible for your safety. I take my own life in my hands in coming here today.'

'Forgive me, sir.' She rubbed her eyes with the backs of her hands in a touching, childish way and tried to smile. 'My teeth hurt me. I can't think clearly when I am in pain.'

The Ambassador leaned across the table.

'We have tried to get Your Highness out of the country but you are too well guarded. It is your duty to submit, Madam, for only you can restore our religion. You must acknowledge your father as Head of the Church.'

'And own myself a bastard? My mother a harlot for all those years? *No.*'

The tears had ceased and her eyes were hard and bright.

'My lady, you can protest privately to Rome that this violation of your conscience is made under duress. His Holiness will absolve you,' Chapuys urged.

'Did my mother ever protest privately to Rome?' she demanded. 'Did Bishop Fisher or Thomas More? They would not sign their names to a falsehood, and neither will I.'

'God regards more the intention than the act,' Chapuys told her. 'But if you don't submit and consent to the King's statutes he will proceed against you.'

'I hate him,' Mary said passionately. 'For what he did to my mother, and for keeping me from my mother when she was dying. And now he locks me up, takes away my confessor, threatens me with the full extremity of the law unless I sign away my birthright.'

She held the document close to her reddened eyes and quoted scornfully.

'"Merciful—compassionate—most blessed." In what is he blessed, Signor? In the imprisonment and deaths of innocent men and women? In the destruction of the Church?'

Chapuys spoke urgently now, with the memory of her mother's obstinacy painfully in his mind.

'Your Highness, for the love of God, sign it—or you are lost.'

'I am lost if I do sign it,' she said wretchedly.

He moved the pen nearer to her hand, but she stared at it dully as if she had forgotten how to write.

'My mother told me,' she said at last, 'how she and my father used to make pilgrimage to the Abbey year after year. They say now that it has been condemned by the Commission, that it will be destroyed, and the monks turned away. If I put my name to this I give my consent to such blasphemies.'

'Sign, Madam,' he begged.

She took the pen, held it poised over the document, then lowered it and burst into a passion of weeping.

There were no tears on the day the Abbey was, by order of the Council, dissolved. Cromwell's men worked efficiently, their faces indifferent to the monks who knelt praying in the wooden pews where they had bent their knees for more years than some of them could count. In their ears sounded the knell of a sledge hammer as it rose and fell upon the casket within which the relics of their patron saint were guarded.

All over England hammers were falling upon shrines. To the monks it was as if the whole world was crumbling. When one of the wreckers jerked his head towards the door, as a signal that it was time for them to leave, they filed out obediently, too conditioned by the habit of submission to protest.

In the courtyard men were packing golden vessels into trunks. Others were piling manuscripts, vestments, copes and missals into the heart of the bonfire lit in the middle of the cobblestones. Smoke from the fire rose up to the roof, now being stripped of its lead, while men perched on high ladders, toiling to remove the great bell which had measured out the minutes of their quiet years.

At the gate an official counted silver into the palm of each monk. Pieces of silver and a cold world in which many of them, without livelihood or families, would sink into a whining beggary.

In his chamber, the Abbot, so old now that his frosty glance could scarcely pierce the width of a room, sank to his knees as a monk entered and whispered to him. After the monk had withdrawn the old man prayed for a few minutes longer and then rose, pulling his aged frame into a standing position, and limping on bare and bunioned feet to his high-backed chair.

The day had apparently come. They had feared it ever since the visit of the Commission, been warned of it after the Commission's Report; and now it was upon them and their lives were as nothing and the future was dark.

The Abbot closed his eyes and saw the past as clear and bright as the first letter of an illuminated psalter. The King had been a red-headed giant of a monarch and Queen Katherine had been small and plump and womanly. They had knelt together in such deep devotion, in such mutual love. And then the black-haired lady with the slanting eyes and the greedy mouth had come, and had poorly concealed her boredom and her distaste for the shabby monks.

And after that everything had changed. Princess Mary was suddenly the Lady Mary and there was a fear in the land, and the shadow of the gibbet darkened the cloisters. It was no longer permissible to give honour to the Pope or to obey the dictates from Rome, for the King was now Head of the Church.

The Abbot had tried to keep up with the times, had tried to remember that Queen Katherine must be referred to as the Princess Dowager of Wales; and preferably not mentioned at all. But even when Nan Bullen had died, the changes had gone on.

There was a new Queen now, not regal or beautiful, but modest and gentle. They said she was a good Catholic and gave generously to charity, but she had not prevented the Commissioners from coming. They had gone everywhere, poking in the backs of cupboards, tasting the soup in the kitchens, upsetting old Brother Anselm who kept the accounts and was not always, it had to be admitted, very reliable in his reckoning.

Now, because of what the Report called 'gross abuses', the Abbey was being pulled down, its treasure burned or carted away, the monks expelled. And with the monks went all the lay people who had made a livelihood out of the work they did on monastery land. Some of them had wives and children to support. There were sick folk in the infirmary, too, and several elderly, crippled men who lived on the premises and gave what help they could in return for their food.

The Abbot's eyes closed in a misery of weariness. It was time for him to leave as well, but he was too tired and too old. There was a life outside the cloister but he couldn't remember it nor recognise himself in its midst.

Men had entered the room and were stripping the

hangings from the walls, lifting the lids of the coffers, smashing the blue-robed Virgin enshrined in the arched glass of the window. One of them, noticing the cowled figure in the high-backed chair, went over to shake the Abbot awake, but paused with fingers still outstretched, for the Abbot would never wake.

A month later the Abbey stood, roofless and eyeless, under a sky which threatened rain. Of the great bonfire only a circle of blackened stones and a little heap of wind-stirred ashes remained. By the gap where the gate had been, a crowd of beggars, rags fluttering, watched the tall, heavily-built man who had dismounted in the lane and now gazed at the desolation with a set, stern face.

In the angle between two walls a woman sat with a child in her arms. The baby had whimpered once or twice and she had drawn her shawl more closely around the thin little body and fever-flushed face. She had walked for many days because the neighbours had told her there would be help at the Abbey, the monks being skilled in the use of herbs and the treatment of disease. But there were no monks and no shelter when she arrived, and she was too tired to go home again.

As the big man turned to leave, the beggars shuffled forwards, their hands stretched out, their eyes anguished and greedy. They were halted by the young man who stood in the lane, holding the two dark-saddled horses.

'Keep from the King!' he called in warning.

They retreated a few paces, their heads lowered, their glances sullen and bewildered. They had heard of the King, of course. He sat upon the throne and wore a crown, had poisoned one wife, cut off the head of another, excommunicated the Pope, and turned out the monks. They found it difficult to relate their idea of the King with the tall, heavily cloaked man who glared about the ravaged place as if it had been responsible for its own destruction.

Henry remounted and rode away without looking back, followed at a little distance by Culpepper. The woman with the child gazed after them, her hands mechanically patting the shawl, her eyes apathetic.

But in the North and in the fens of Lincolnshire apathy flared up into anger, and anger was expressed at first in a low rumbling of discontent like the thunder that heralds a storm. They gathered around their firesides, leaned whispering across tavern tables, padded through the darkness with makeshift weapons tucked in their belts. Their talk was secret, treasonable, dangerous.

'Who can give me a good reason why the King should be Head of the Church?'

'There is no good reason, save that Parliament made a law.'

'Sir Thomas More asked once if Parliament could pass a law to say God was not God. He was told they could not, and he answered that neither could they make the King Head of the Church.'

'But they deprived More of his own head, didn't they?'

'And Fisher too.'

'And poisoned the real Queen to set up the Concubine. Princess Mary is kept close prisoner now, because she will not say she is a bastard.'

'And the monasteries are all being torn down or made into mansions for Cromwell's cronies.'

'While we lack alms and hospitals and labouring work in the cloisters.'

'The Faith is being destroyed all over England.'

'Every time an Abbey is pulled down Christ is crucified afresh.'

Whispers in the darkness, and then the darkness seared by tongues of flame as beacon answered beacon from one hilltop to the next. The men of the north came from their villages, from their hamlets, from the bleak moors, tramping with steady, unrelenting purpose through the autumn days. These were mainly uneducated men, rough of visage, rude of speech. Their arms were crude and their banners unhemmed and daubed with ploughs and horns, and the five wounds of Christ. And over them lay a certain, simple nobility as potent as the innocence of some dumb beast. For this was a pilgrimage, not against Turks or heathens but against those who had twisted and despoiled the Faith for their own selfish ends.

They swung southward through Lincoln, collecting more supporters as they came. And the tramp of their feet echoed below the leaves that fluttered, blood-red, from the arching oaks.

CHAPTER EIGHT

Messengers rode sweating through the night and panted up the staircase of Hampton Court to present news of the rising to the authorities. The King glared round his hastily assembled Council.

'*How* many, Cromwell?'

'Thirty thousand of them, Your Grace,' Cromwell answered promptly, without bothering to consult the document he held. 'They march south through Lincoln, demanding that you suppress no more abbeys and that you return to the old order. God's Quarrel, they call it.'

'God's Quarrel.' Henry echoed the words reflectively; then asked abruptly, 'What other matters do they propose?'

'No taxation.' Cromwell glanced at the document and continued smoothly. 'And the removal of certain counsellors from Your Grace's service.'

'The Vicar General for one,' Norfolk said with a look of loathing.

Cromwell returned the look in double measure.

Henry chewed his underlip and spoke with icy calm. 'I have never read that a Prince's council should be appointed by rude, ignorant and common people, have you, my lords?'

The question was purely rhetorical for, before any one could answer, the storm broke over their heads.

'Chirst in Heaven!' Henry shouted, 'don't we know after twenty-seven years how to govern our kingdom! Am I a puppet to be jerked on strings pulled by men of no learning, no wit, no political judgment! Are peasants now to decide what laws are to be passed, what decisions taken in Council! Men it seems have decided to become the masters! *Suffolk.*'

'Your Grace?' The burly duke put on his most loyally obedient expression.

'Take a hundred thousand men, horse and foot. The Secretary has the list of musters. Choose veterans who fought with me in France, or at Flodden. My lord Beauchamp,' he flung a hand towards Edward Seymour, 'shall go with you.'

'Your Grace.'

The Queen's brother bowed gravely, his long face pulled into its habitual expression of melancholy.

'Make an example of these lewd subjects and reduce this land to due civility. I want no quarter.' Henry thumped a side table until the goblets on it rattled. 'We will follow within the week.'

The prospect of riding into battle again pleased him so much that his rage momentarily faded. A stab of pain along his thigh as he brought his foot down too heavily to the ground brought it flooding back, however, and he limped out angrily, thrusting aside Culpepper's helping hand.

It didn't sweeten his temper to be greeted by a downcast and silent wife. Jane heard the news of the rebellion with a look of horror on her face, but the horror was not, it appeared, at the notion of commoners objecting to his lawful authority.

'The poor men!' she breathed. 'So many of them will be hurt or killed.'

'I too will ride out,' he said in surprised displeasure.

'Is that wise? Your leg——' She looked concerned.

'I am still capable of sitting a horse!' Henry said testily. 'You had best swallow your arguments and help me into something more suited to a campaign.'

Katherine would have continued to argue; Anne would have flown into a temper. This third, gentler wife merely coloured a little and followed him meekly into his chamber where she stood, hands clasped and eyelids downcast, while Culpepper brought in a change of clothing.

His attendant dismissed, Henry brought his attention back to the Queen, noting how her hands trembled as she handed him his fresh shirt. He had a desire to hold and comfort her.

'You maintain a marvellous obstinate silence, Madam,' he observed.

'I am bound to obey and serve you, sir,' she said at last in a dull, flat little voice.

'Your silence does me no service!' he retorted.

She bit her lip and knelt before him with his riding boots in her hand.

After a moment, Henry said loudly as if he were still addressing his Council, 'They have always given me their support and I am ready to hear any just complaints, but not open resistance.'

'Sir, if I may speak——' Jane fiddled nervously with the lace on her dress.

'I told you to,' Henry said with deliberate patience.

'I can only think——' She hesitated again, then rushed on, 'Sir, I bear great love for you, but I believe this to be God's judgment for putting down the abbeys.'

'Oh don't be simple, Jane.' He pulled on the second boot and scowled down at her. 'Did you read the report of the visitations?'

She shook her head, and her wordlessness released in the King a final anger.

'Well, Parliament did, Madam—and there was one loud cry of "Down with them, the monks, the abbeys, the church"—my church for which I am responsible in the sight of God.'

Jane had risen and was taking a cloak from among the half-dozen laid across the bed. Her voice was muffled in its folds.

'Will you wear this one, sir?' she enquired shakily.

As Henry shrugged himself into the velvet he could not avoid her brimming eyes.

'You're such a gentle thing, you dare hardly speak, and now I have cowed you. But the abbeys were not above reproach, Jane, believe me.'

'Sir, I am willing to believe some few instances of corruption——' she began.

'Some!' he interrupted her violently. 'Why, the entire system is—No, no; go on. I'll hear you out.'

At another time he might have smiled at the resolute manner in which she put up her chin and clenched her small fingers, but her words fed his wrath.

'I think there was much good done by them, sir. In husbandry and in learning. I have seen friars in Wiltshire.' Her fingers agitated his sleeve. 'Our Franciscans —providing comfort for the homeless, visiting the sick in all weathers without thought for their own welfare or reward. Now they themselves are homeless without the means to live. Your people, sir, of the selfsame religion.'

'Madam, your monasteries are the strongholds of Romish fraud and superstition,' Henry said tightly. 'From this time Christianity, not monkery, is to be the law of this land.'

'But your promise was to reform, sir, not to destroy,' she reminded him.

So, she was no different from Katherine and Anne! Lacking the obstinacy of the one and the temper of the other, Jane was still disobedient and stubborn, refusing support to her wedded lord.

Henry rounded on her, his face swollen and blotched with rage.

'Reform? Reform men who sell the Church's plate, jewels and timber for their own profit? Monks drinking till ten or twelve of the clock, many at cards or dice or found in bed with their drabs? Nuns who support their bastards out of church funds? The list is endless, Madam, and beyond redemption. Your monks, Madam, whose business is the cure of souls, do more traffic in images and relics—God's coat here, Our Lady's smock there—saints' clothing to help barren women; trumpery to bring rain or grow corn or prevent weeds! And you believe such things?'

He whirled about and wrenched up the lid of a chest, lifting out an opaque glass phial.

'Do you know this, Madam?' He thrust the object before her. 'You should. Cromwell brought it for my instruction. *Your* Blood of Christ. From Hailes, Madam. Look well now.'

She had turned her face aside, but he pulled at her shoulder, his nails digging into her flesh, his voice thundering in her shrinking ears.

'*Look at it!* It's dark—you see nothing, do you? You have not paid for absolution. But give me your coin, Madam, and we turn the hidden spring so that you can see the blood so that you are absolved—except that it is the blood of a domestic duck which the monks renew every week! Now—will you still make a God of the Pope's creatures, Madam?'

Jane wept silently, and his anger had gone, washed away by her tears and by the memory that came to him of the day they had walked together through the fields near Wolf Hall.

She had been happy then. Her face had glowed when she told him how she had visited Hailes many times. And he had taken the glow from her face, had attacked her deepest and most sincere beliefs. Shamefaced, he put down the phial.

'It is not what it seems, you see.'

But she went on crying, hopelessly and helplessly as if she would never stop. He went over to her and knelt with his arms about her waist and his head pressed into her skirt. Words limped from him as if their very meaning was bruised.

'Forgive me. I'm a rough man—rough tempered. I wouldn't have shown it but—Jane, don't make me doubt. Ever! When I doubt I can only strike out in blindness. I don't know what I say or do. Am I sick perhaps, in my mind? Am I?'

Not until the actual words were spoken did he recognise the secret and terrible fear that gripped him. Then he felt her small hands clasping him tightly and her voice, blurred by tears, comforting.

'No, sir. Oh no, sir.'

'I feel old,' he moaned. 'So old.'

'You must rest, sir,' she soothed.

'I will, I will,' he promised, rising with difficulty, and leaning on her. She was so slight that it was like depending on a child. He straightened up and looked down at her, his self-esteem returning as he saw her fragility.

'First we must put down these rebels or lose our throne,' he said briskly, and caught her to him, holding her closely and crying out, almost in despair. 'Oh, Jane, if only you and I had met before. I doubt now that we shall ever have any children.'

'Sir, we are both young,' she began, but he had released her and was shouting for Culpepper to have his horse brought round.

When he had gone she sat down on the bed among the disordered cloaks and watched the slow tears drip through her fingers. In her mind a slow procession of monks moved away from a ruined and deserted abbey.

Another royal lady wept as news of the rebellion filtered through to the prison-palace of Hunsdon. At twenty, Mary had the nervous, tense look of a woman much older to whom life had not been kind. Her stiff little figure had a wariness about it and her mouth was guarded. In contrast her eyes, puffed by sleepless nights and constant headache, had an expression of affectionate yearning.

The destruction of the abbeys had been like the last wail of mourning for her mother. Queen Katherine had spent much of her time in prayer before one shrine or another. Now she was dead and the very buildings where she had worshipped had become storehouses for rats, private dwellings, or gaunt ruins silhouetted against the sky.

From time to time little bands of dispossessed monks and nuns begged for charity at the gates of Hunsdon. Mary had given what she could and been so furiously rated for it in a letter from Cromwell that she had spent a week in nervous tears. It was now treason, it seemed, to help those of her own faith who were in need. It was wicked to obey the commands of the Holy Father in Rome or to pay homage to the relics of the saints. The world had been turned upside-down for a woman who had produced nothing more than another daughter.

When Mary looked at her tiny, red-haired half-sister, she felt unwilling love struggle with remembered hatred. She must always bear in mind the fact that both she and Elizabeth were motherless now, and that a new Queen sat upon the throne.

The Lady Jane Seymour had been one of Mary's closest friends when she was at Court. They said she was a gentle Queen and that her heart still clung to the old faith. The *true* faith, thought Mary, and her lips took on a bitter curve as she glanced across to where the document lay ready for her signature.

She knew its wording by heart for she had read it over and over ever since Chapuys had first shown it to her, but familiarity did not lessen her shuddering contempt when she saw again the lies to which she must swear before she could be admitted to her father's Court.

And if she still refused to sign they were likely to accuse her of complicity in the rebellion. The walls of the Tower loomed in her frightened mind, but stronger than the dread of dungeons was the overwhelming loneliness that cast down her spirits.

Her father had loved her once. He had pulled off her cap to show her pretty hair and boasted to the Ambassador that she never cried. Once, so long ago that it was no more than faded lavender in the store chest of her childhood, there had been a garden full of butterflies and she had chased them and the red-haired giant who was her father had laughed.

She remembered that great laugh filling the garden. Surely, if she could remember a time so far removed, her father might recall it too and feel some lingering tenderness. But, surrounded as he was by those evil men, who filled their hands with the Church's gold and did to death loyal men and women, it was likely that he would forget his elder daughter, perhaps hear of her arrest and death without a qualm. He had loved Nan Bullen wildly once, and now she was Nan Lackhead.

Slowly, her eyes fixed upon the document, Mary crossed to the table, and picked up her pen. It is so easy, she thought, to sign away one's soul in return for a little love and so hard to forgive oneself the sin.

Yet when at last the permission came to return to Court, happiness and terror were strangely mingled. In the swaying litter as they journeyed to Hampton Court, if Mary closed her eyes, she could picture again the tall, splendid figure whose approval she craved. When she opened her eyes she could see the blackening corpses that hung from the trees on each side of the road. The rebels hung, stinking and crow-pecked, under the winter sky and Mary crossed herself and leaned back within the curtains of her litter.

Others who passed along took no notice of the death-fringed lanes. Hangings were already commonplace and burnings becoming so. The rich and titled were usually beheaded, and if one was fortunate enough to get a good place then there was often excellent sport, better than a bear-baiting, or cock-fighting.

The carter pulled his horse's head towards the ditch and watched incuriously as the leather-curtained litter with its escort of guards passed by. Some important person was evidently bound for the Court. He was going the same way himself. As he approached the toll-gate he raised his voice hoarsely.

'Quail and cherries for the Queen's Grace!'

Lesser women who had fancies when they were breeding had to make do with what their husbands could afford. Royal ladies could order quail and cherries out of season. The carter grinned, jerking on the reins as the guard emerged yawning from the toll-gate.

Within the State Chamber, hung with its scarlet and gold, lit by shafts of pale sunlight that dipped down to the rush-lights and the blazing fire, the Queen sat on the daïs next to her husband.

Jane had already been sick twice that morning and was horribly afraid that she would be sick again if she didn't escape soon into the fresh air. The bright gowns of her ladies merged before her eyes into a rainbow of jarring contrasts and the chattering voices around her were as shrill and meaningless as the chirping of crickets. She closed her eyes for a moment and, opening them in time to catch Henry's look of concern, forced a faint smile to her lips.

'It is a trifle warm,' she said hesitantly, but Henry, apparently reassured by the smile, nodded absently and fixed his eyes upon the great door where the Chamberlain waited. There was no knowing, Jane thought in sudden fear, how he would react when Mary arrived.

When the signed document had been shown to him, he had seemed pleased and told Cromwell that Mary appeared to be learning sense at last. But later, talking to Jane, he had begun to doubt whether his daughter's change of heart were genuine.

Why could he not accept matters and allow them all to be comfortable together? It was impossible to gauge his reactions to anything, and when his leg throbbed or his head ached he was likely to take offence at the smallest thing.

The hum of conversation was growing louder and several heads were turned towards the door. On many faces there was a wary excitement, for, while the King could be difficult, Mary was also the child of Katherine of Aragon, a very stubborn and conscience-bound woman. A clash of wills between father and daughter would be dangerous—but stimulating.

One late arrival shouldered his way towards Bishop Gardiner, rumbling as he came.

'So the Queen has had her way.'

Gardiner gave the Duke of Norfolk an elegant little bow and a brief upward glance as he replied without inflection, 'Yes, my lord, the meek shall inherit the earth.'

Norfolk rubbed the side of his nose.

'That's not original, is it?' he enquired doubtfully.

'It was first spoken many centuries ago,' the Bishop began.

'Oh, *history*!'

Norfolk gave a shrug and changed his growl into a cough, as the Chamberlain tapped his staff three times upon the floor.

The ladies were spreading their skirts wide in readiness for the formal curtsey. Norfolk moved to take his place by the Duke of Suffolk.

'Interesting to see who can pretend the best,' he mumbled.

'Well, she is *his* daughter,' Suffolk returned from behind a beefy hand.

In the doorway a small, erect figure sank into a curtsey. Mary's face was so pale that she looked as if she were about to faint. Her ladies, ranged behind her, kept their eyes demurely downcast, but Mary's eyes were fixed imploringly upon the King, who sat immovable as stone, though his cheeks had flushed.

Halfway across the room she curtsied again, her knees shaking so violently that her skirt fluttered as if she stood in a breeze. A third curtsey brought her to the foot of the daïs and then she sank down gratefully, her small hands tightly clasped together, her voice harsh with repressed feeling.

'Sire—your wholly humble and obedient servant asks your blessing.'

Such a pretty child she had been, Henry remembered. Such a darting, dancing, elf of a thing. And the black-haired witch had kept her away from him, ordered her to act as handmaid to the Lady Elizabeth.

Henry rose as the Queen's knuckles tensed on the arm of her chair. His voice was rich with paternal feeling long denied as he raised her gently.

'My dear child, you are most welcome.'

Jane let out her breath in a quivering little sigh of relief and joined the embraced pair with her own hands out-stretched in greeting.

'Mary, my dear. Welcome.'

The girl was trembling still but a tinge of colour had returned to her face. Jane held her old companion warmly, trying to instil into her a feeling of confidence and security. Henry, noting his daughter's fine-drawn, tense expression, looked round for somewhere to fix the blame and caught sight of Norfolk.

'And some of you wanted me to put this jewel to death,' he said.

Norfolk's mouth had fallen open, as he vainly tried to remember when he had ever said any such thing.

'That were great pity, sir,' Jane said quickly, 'to have lost your chief jewel of England.'

'Nay, sweetheart, but Edward—Edward.' The King smote her lightly with the palm of his hand on her stomach.

'It will be a fine boy. Her Grace looks so well,' Mary plucked up courage to remark.

'The astrologers declare it is a male child.'

Henry frowned slightly, remembering occasions when the astrologers had been wrong before.

'And Edward is a fine name for a Prince of Wales to bear,' Jane said.

She knew what was in Henry's mind, and felt faint and sick again. Always, beneath her joy in the coming child, ran the undercurrent of terror. Two previous wives had borne daughters and stillborn sons and those wives were dead now, one harried to her grave, the other flung there in two pieces.

'It would please me if Lady Elizabeth could also visit the Court,' she said nervously.

'And she shall be brought, sweetheart,' Henry said promptly. 'They tell me she is a forward minx.'

'Very forward, Your Grace,' Mary said eagerly. 'She has some trouble with her back-teeth, but they are through now and she is a sweetling of a child.'

'It will be good for Edward to have companions,' Henry agreed.

He shot his wife a fond glance. Jane was an excellent woman. She lacked Katherine's strong will, being ever gentle and yielding, and there was in her none of the sparkle that Nan had possessed. There were even times when she bored him a little, but he would always love her.

'We will engage Mother Jack as nurse for the boy. She is highly commended,' he said, and saw Jane's eyes fill with tears, no doubt at this evidence of the interest he took in the child. She was a loving, sentimental creature, holding hands now with Mary as if, in some fanciful way, they gained strength from each other.

CHAPTER NINE

Jane had been wandering in green fields, seeking flowers to weave into a garland. She would hang the garland in the church and wait for a young man to pluck it and win her as his lady. But a King rode past, tall and shining, and took down the flowers and in taking them down tore at the foundations of the church until the walls cracked and crumbled and the lead melted from the roof and black-beetles scurried from the wooden pews.

The King lifted his great foot and crushed them and she saw then that they were not insects but monks and nuns, reduced and vulnerable, and she cried out to the King begging him to save them; but he laughed, swinging her up before him on the saddle and throwing the wreath over her head. And the flowers came apart in her hair and fell, petal by petal, each one turning into a little spike that burrowed into her flesh until she sobbed aloud in her agony.

Then she remembered that the days of flower gathering were over and she was bearing the King's child. She wanted the child desperately for Henry's sake, but also because she dreaded the curse of barrenness. Words broke from her lips, spilling out into the warm room. Somebody wiped her face with a cloth and then the pain swooped upon her again and she heard her own voice crying out, begging it to cease.

Edward Seymour, walking in the corridor with Archbishop Cranmer, heard his sister's muffled cry and twitched his robe higher as if to cover his ears and shut out the sound. He wished he dare suggest that they move to a more remote part of the palace, but the

King had ordered them to wait upon him here, and Henry was not in a mood to be approached with trivial requests.

He stood now, half-turned away from them, his square-toed shoe beating the flagstones, his lips pressed tight within his fringe of beard. He too had heard the sound, and the thought of what lay behind the closed door twisted in him like a knife. Jane was so small, as narrow-hipped as a child. He could circle her waist with his two hands.

'It's been thirty hours!' he cried out, loudly and angrily.

Cranmer and Seymour paused in their walk, their faces compassionate and embarrassed. As if in response to Henry's cry the door opened and Lady Rochford emerged, her face tense and drawn with all the secret excitement of bad news in her eyes.

'Well?' Henry barked the word but his jaw was shaking.

'Her Grace is begging us to save the child, sir,' Lady Rochford told him. 'The midwife says it is a boy.'

An heir for the throne, a Prince of the Blood Royal to wear the crown when Henry mouldered in the earth! For a moment wild exultation rose in the King's heart. Then the full meaning of Lady Rochford's words sank in and he stared at her in piteous entreaty.

'It is the Queen's wish, sir. May I tell the physicians to proceed?' she asked.

He nodded slowly, his mouth working soundlessly. The door opened again and closed behind Lady Rochford.

'My sister is stronger than she looks,' Edward Seymour said uneasily. 'It was Jane who nursed us through our coughs and colds when we were young together at Wolf Hall.'

'We can only wait and pray. There is always hope,'

Cranmer murmured.

The King heeded neither of them. He had turned again to the window and was staring out at the sky as if he intended to force Heaven to change its mind. For this surely was the cruellest irony of all, that the wife he loved best should be taken from him in return for a son.

Within the birth-chamber Jane moaned faintly as her limbs were stretched to allow her to expel the child. This then was how the monks had suffered as they were torn on the rack. And the same punishment was being meted out to her because she had failed to save them.

Her lips shaped her husband's name, but the word remained unspoken, because it was Henry who caused her suffering, and a cry to him would be as futile as a bat blundering along empty cloisters.

She was astonished to find herself still alive when Lady Rochford took the squirming bundle from the physician and stepped out into the corridor with it. They were crowding about her, their voices rapid with relief, their eyes bright with no understanding of the agony she had experienced.

And then she was not in a bed but on a high couch and there were choking clouds of incense all around her and the glitter of golden ornaments in her eyes. She was in a chapel and for a moment she believed it to be the chapel at Hailes, and rejoiced. Then she remembered that this was the royal chapel and that on this day they were naming a royal heir. Later she would ask to see the child, but now she was tired, so tired that the scene blurred before her eyes and the sound of the trumpets began to fade into the lowing of cattle as she picked up her skirts and ran out into the green meadow.

Prince Edward lay snug and secure in the carved cradle over which Mother Jack bent in loving concern.

In the street people stood silently, many of them weeping. Good Queen Jane, as they were already calling her, would be buried at Windsor, but the King would not attend the funeral. He had not attended the funerals of his other wives either and already rumour whispered through the city.

Katherine had borne a daughter, and been secretly poisoned. Nan Bullen had borne a daughter, and been executed. Jane Seymour had, by order of the King, her living son torn from her body that there might be an heir for England even though the mother died.

At Hampton Court, Cromwell padded along the corridor to the antechamber where Norfolk and Cranmer waited with Suffolk and Bishop Gardiner. A little apart from them Edward Seymour stood with bowed head. Jane had been his sister as well as his Queen and he had never forgotten to love her even when he was energetically furthering his own ambitions.

Old animosities were forgotten in the relief of the moment as Norfolk hurried forward.

'Thank God you've come! You are the one man to whom the King might listen. We have urged His Grace to accept God's pleasure in taking the Queen, and to comfort himself in the boy, but——'

'Is the boy healthy?' Cromwell asked.

They looked doubtfully at one another.

'He'll have to be nursed,' Suffolk said.

Cromwell's reply was brusquely practical. 'Then the King must take a new wife.'

'God's blood, man!' Suffolk darted a look towards Edward Seymour, who shivered without lifting his head.

'*You* tell him that,' Norfolk gibed, his natural dislike of an upstart returning in full measure.

'Where is he?' There was a tinge of insolence in the question as if Cromwell had expected the King to greet his arrival.

Bishop Gardiner nodded towards the door of the royal bedchamber, as Cromwell took a step forward.

'His Grace will see nobody,' the Bishop warned.

The minister's brief and contemptuous smile as he moved towards the door said clearly, 'His Grace will see *me*.'

He knocked twice, sharply, and then under their half-envious, half-admiring gaze opened the door, and went in.

The room was in semi-darkness with shutters closed and the dying ashes of an October fire faintly lighting the gloom. The King sat near the high bed, staring at it as if he were trying to conjure up his wife's frail form among the uncrumpled sheets and blankets. There was such an emptiness of grief in the room.

'Your Grace?' Cromwell said gently.

There was no response from the motionless figure in the high-backed chair.

Cromwell tried again in a slightly louder tone.

'Good-day to Your Grace.'

Into the silence of the darkened room Henry's voice fell at last, heavy and rough with pain.

'Have you seen my son?'

'Yes, indeed,' Cromwell lied.

'He'll live, won't he?' Henry asked. 'He *must* live, or there's no reason for it all.'

'Everything shall be done for his governance,' Cromwell said reassuringly. 'In the meantime, I would urge Your Grace to think of providing for a new wife.'

The silence was terrible now, chilling the blood as if winter were come to hang icicles from the eaves. Yet when Henry spoke again his voice was low.

'Leave me, Cromwell.'

'Your Grace——'

'I would be private,' Henry said as if the other had not begun to speak.

'Sir, we must consider the boy's condition,' Cromwell persisted.

But the figure in the chair swung round violently, crying hoarsely, 'Leave me! Would you rub salt in my wound? I shall never marry again. Now go! Go before I do you some hurt!'

At least, thought Cromwell as he left the room, His Grace has been roused to anger.

But, left alone, Henry sank into apathy again. The child for which he had longed throughout the years was born at last, but as God gave with one hand so he snatched away with the other. Little, gentle Jane was dead and he would never love another woman as he had loved her. He was too old to love again, as if her dying had sapped all his youth.

Such a golden youth as he had been, riding against Suffolk in the tiltyard! He recalled the jarring of the long spear against his half-closed helmet, the splinters flying before his face, the reeling sky. And now a splinter had entered his heart and the pain was greater than he had ever known.

But the months moved inexorably on and there were state duties to attend, and the child thrived. He bent his mind to the care of his kingdom and the governance of his son, and was glad when the next spring had passed and snowdrops no longer brought the tears to his eyes.

Care for his son's welfare had become the paramount object in his life, but the existence of a child was precarious, as Henry had sad reason to know. Even while he dandled the infant on his sound leg, the knowledge that this was his only male heir spoiled the pleasure of the moment.

'His food is tasted?' anxiously he enquired of his daughter. 'Everything he eats?'

Mary, fulfilling a vicarious motherhood towards her small half-brother, soothed her father reassuringly.

'Yes, sir. Everything.'

'He bites his lip,' Henry worried, studying the small, puckered face.

'He's only cutting another tooth. Mother Jack shall rub rosemary jelly on it.'

'Yes, at once. Take him, and let it be done at once.'

The King's indulgent smile as he watched Mary carry the prince from the apartment twisted into pain as his leg began to throb again. He eased it higher on the cushion and wished suddenly that he had a wife who would make him forget the nagging discomfort.

He brightened slightly as he remembered that tentative negotiations for a new marriage were being pursued. It would, of course, be a purely political alliance for he could never fall in love again, but it would be necessary for the lady to be of childbearing age, and he was not so old that her looks and bearing didn't matter.

As Cromwell had said, it was the King's duty to beget as many male heirs as possible for the future defence of the realm.

When Cromwell and Secretary Wriothesley ushered in the French Ambassador, Henry forgot the ache in his leg for sheer delight at the thought of the battle of wills that lay ahead. The audience began, however, with the usual polite enquiries as to the healths of their Graces of France and England.

'I passed His Grace Prince Edward as I came,' Castillon remarked.

'He's a merry boy,' Henry said proudly. 'Did you not think so?'

'The fairest child that I ever saw, Your Majesty,' the Frenchman said promptly.

Henry reddened with pleasure and leaned forward slightly, eager to begin the real business of the meeting.

'About Madame de Longueville——' he ventured

hopefully.

'Alas, the lady is already promised to Scotland,' Castillon regretted.

'She was a fine woman, to judge from her portrait,' Henry said wistfully.

'If Your Majesty would consider her sister or the Princess Madeleine?'

'Monsieur, I am big in person, and I have need of a big wife,' Henry said abruptly, remembering that Jane had been so tiny that the birth of her child had killed her.

'It is so difficult to estimate,' said Castillon apologetically.

'I know, you shall bring them all to Calais for me,' Henry said brightly.

'I fear it would not be possible,' Castillon said stiffly, 'to trot them out like horses. But if Your Majesty wishes to send someone to look at them——'

'No, no, I must see them for myself,' Henry interrupted, forgetting tact in his desire to impress upon a foreigner that Englishmen were not in the habit of buying pigs in pokes. 'Whose opinion can I trust above my own? What pleases one may not please another. I must see them for myself and *hear* them sing.'

'Perhaps Your Majesty would like to try them one after the other and keep the one you found most agreeable,' Castillon said.

Henry gave a little embarrassed laugh and waved his hand feebly.

'It is an idea, Monsieur,' he said. 'We will have to think about it.'

'Your Majesty.' Castillon bowed without troubling to hide the contempt in his eyes as he withdrew.

Henry heaved to his feet, grasping for the stick which leaned always within reach.

'These Frenchmen,' he said, 'have no sense of humour. They never realise when one is making a joke.

The Italians now have a lighter, gayer touch.'

He had drifted over to the table on which lay a portrait of the young Duchess of Milan.

'Young, intelligent and beautiful,' he mused. 'Now there's a woman—and you say she favours me, eh?'

'Sir, the Duchess sings your praises but is entirely obedient to the Emperor,' Wriothesley said.

'Then why does he keep me waiting for an answer?' Henry demanded.

'I don't believe he means an alliance,' Cromwell said bluntly. 'His terms are too high.'

'His grandfather was the same,' Henry said wryly.

'If I may suggest to Your Grace——' Cromwell began.

'Yes, yes, Crum, a Protestant league!' Henry tapped his stick impatiently. 'You never stop suggesting it.'

'It would restore the balance,' Cromwell said stubbornly, 'and drive a wedge between France and the Empire.'

'But it commits us; it commits us,' Henry frowned thoughtfully.

'It would demonstrate Your Grace's independence of Papist alliances.'

'True, but it would mean a Protestant marriage. I am no friend to the Lutherans.'

'Nor, I believe, to the Pope,' his minister said slyly.

'Bishop of Rome,' Henry corrected automatically. 'You're quite right, of course. England needs neither France nor the Emperor. The little picture you had of the princess of Cleves—Sophia?'

'Sophia is the married one,' Cromwell reminded him. 'The miniature is of her younger sister, Anne. There was a likeness of the third sister, Amelia, too.'

'Let me see the picture of Anne again.'

The King put out his hand for the small ivory box in which the portrait rested. It was, he thought as he held it to the light, an attractive face, calm and sweet with a gentleness about the lips.

'Everyone praises her virtue, and her beauty,' Cromwell said eagerly.

'All my prospective brides are praised for their virtue and beauty,' Henry said gloomily. 'But is it a likeness, eh?'

'Master Holbein has a high reputation,' Cromwell assured him.

'And I can scarcely journey to Cleves to inspect the lady for myself,' Henry regretted. 'And mere beauty is not, after all, the first consideration.'

'But the people of England will expect a graceful Queen,' Wriothesley interposed.

'True, and one must strive to please the people,' Henry agreed. 'But is she tall? One cannot tell from this.'

'The princess is tall and stately. That is generally agreed,' Wriothesley said.

'Young?'

'Twenty-four, Your Grace. Healthy and lively, but past the silly season.'

'What of her talents? Is she musical? Does she sing and play the lute?'

'I believe not, sir,' Cromwell said reluctantly, 'but her needlework is unsurpassed.'

Another Anne had sung, deep and husky, to the melody of the lute and tossed back her long hair, slanting her eyes towards the gypsy who played.

'Shall we knit with her, then?' Henry enquired, so loudly that the other two looked at him in surprise. 'What a blow to the Empire and to France? To ask them both for brides and to take neither! I will take this Anne of Cleves and raise a new alliance with the Protestant states. You will send somebody to open the negotiations at once; and I want them speedily concluded.'

'Yes, Your Grace.' If his head had depended on it,

Cromwell could not have hidden his delight.

'A political alliance is more important than the dictates of the heart,' Henry said gravely. 'But I would have liked the Duchess—those dimples.'

His gaze strayed regretfully to the table on which the portrait of Christina of Milan lay.

'Sir, Anne of Cleves surpasses the Duchess as the sun does the moon,' Cromwell said, but Henry had stumped out and his words reached only the Secretary's ear.

'The Duchess told me in confidence that she would only marry him if she had two heads,' Wriothesley grinned.

Cromwell permitted himself an answering smile. He had, after all, good reason to congratulate himself. This marriage would provide the basis for a new and exciting shift of power in foreign affairs. It would also be a personal victory against the Duke of Norfolk, who regarded Cromwell as an insolent upstart.

Henry had reached the end of the corridor when he saw Mary coming towards him. As always, his daughter tensed a little before she sank into a curtsey, and, as always, he greeted her with a joviality that never rang quite true.

'We have been discussing this question of my marriage.'

She made no reply.

'It is necessary for the safety of the realm that I take another wife,' he said sharply. 'The prince is very small and much may happen. We hope and pray that it does not, of course, but one must look ahead. France and the Emperor have both offered various ladies, but I have a taste for a new alliance—with the princess of Cleves.'

'A Protestant alliance,' Mary said in a small voice and made a slight gesture as if she were brushing insects off her dress.

'A new political arrangement,' Henry corrected testily. 'Anne of Cleves is twenty-four, young enough to bear children, but old enough to have put aside any foolish, romantic notions.'

He remembered suddenly that Mary was just twenty-four and felt acute embarrassment colour his face.

'She may feel a trifle lonely in a strange country at first,' he said swiftly, 'so we must make her welcome when she comes.'

'Of course, Your Grace. And I shall pray for your happiness,' Mary said in the same small, tight voice.

'Of course, of course.' He patted her awkwardly on the shoulder. 'We must find a husband for you very soon. One of the German princes perhaps?'

'I am in no great haste to wed,' Mary said stiffly.

'In a year or so, perhaps. We have seen little enough of you at Court recently.'

He coughed again, averting his gaze from the clear eyes that said plainly, 'It was not my fault that I was not here.'

'Pray that I find happiness with this new wife,' he begged suddenly. 'I found it with Jane but she was taken from me so suddenly and Edward is too small to lack a mother.'

Mary curtsied silently and moved in the direction of the chapel. When she was not supervising the upbringing of the prince she spent much of her time kneeling before the altar. Sometimes she repeated the set prayers that she had learned from her mother. There was a discipline in them that calmed her spirit, so that she could almost fancy herself a child again listening to Queen Katherine's voice prompting her in the harder passages.

But always another voice intruded, the husky voice of the Bullen whore as she cried out, loudly enough for Mary to hear, 'Give her a box on the ears now and then for the bastard she is.'

Nan Bullen had flaunted black satin and eaten roast pheasant by leaping firelight, while Queen Katherine had died in a shabby room, poisoned it was believed by her successful rival. But three months later Nan's head had been stricken from her shoulders, so she had not enjoyed her triumph for very long. Yet she had died bravely, they said, never admitting her guilt but imploring Mary to be kind to the little Elizabeth.

Better not to think of that. Better to think of Queen Jane who had brought Mary back to court and been more sister than stepmother. The physicians had almost torn Jane apart in order to deliver her son.

One son for England and now the King wanted another and had asked for his daughter's prayers. Mary's lips moved silently but it was the unknown princess from Cleves for whom she begged mercy and a measure of content.

THE TIME OF THE MARE

❉❉❉

❉❉ CHAPTER TEN ❉❉

The princess had never been so nervous in her life. She had almost reached the stage of believing she was doomed to live out her days as a spinster in the royal palace of Cleves. And spinning, thought Anne surveying her reflection with a little grimace, is one talent that I do possess.

Both she and her sisters had been carefully trained in the skills of needlework and cooking, but Amelia was sometimes a little careless and left her work unfinished. Amelia was so pretty that she was usually forgiven.

Yet of the two portraits that Master Holbein had painted it was the one of Anne that had found favour in the King's eyes. It was Anne who had been fitted for the bridal gown and been chosen to make the sea-voyage that had brought her to this foreign country where she now lodged in a town with the unpronounceable name of Rochester, waiting for her bridegroom.

When Anne thought of her bridegroom she trembled a little and felt the colour mount in her cheeks. They had told her that King Henry was one of the most powerful monarchs in the world. He spoke many languages and played many instruments and could tire out five horses in one day's hunt.

They had told her that this marriage would bind together all the Protestant states in a new and powerful alliance. But she had heard other things, whispered by her ladies when they thought she wasn't listening.

The King's first wife had been locked away and poisoned, his second had been beheaded, and his third had been allowed to die in order that a living son might be born.

If Anne failed to please him—but she closed the thought firmly out of her mind. She was a tall, strong woman with excellent eyes and teeth, even if her features were large, and her skin pitted. And she had covered her own dark hair with a yellow wig because it was known that the King liked blondes.

In the corridor beyond, Henry leaned upon his stick, adjusting his cap and fiddling with his newly trimmed and perfumed beard. Had there been more time he would have lost a little weight by ordering his physicians to put him on a strict diet, but he had been so eager to meet his bride that he had ridden to the Bishop's palace on the spur of the moment. Cromwell and Wriothesley had accompanied him and Tom Culpepper, grown into a handsome youth, stood near, with the magnificent sable fur that Henry had chosen as his greeting gift draped over his arm.

In the background Cranmer hovered with the usual anxiety lengthening his face. The expression was, if anything, slightly more pronounced than was customary—the Archbishop having already met the bride.

'Well, where is she?' Henry demanded. 'Where is this paragon?'

'As Your Grace was not expected, the Princess Anne and her ladies are hardly prepared, sir,' Cranmer said nervously.

'Such praise runs ahead of her that we cannot abide our impatience,' Henry told him. 'Where is she?'

'In there, sir.' Unhappily Cranmer indicated the door.

'I will burst in upon her like an unexpected spring,' Henry cried, suiting action to his words as he thrust open the door and stumped in, his voice ringing. 'We would nourish love with a suitable gift—of——'

His voice trailed away and he came to a dead stop in

the middle of the room, staring in bewilderment at the group of ladies in their round-skirted gowns and prim bonnets. His arrival had caused a sudden stillness, and then a high twittering broke out as the strangely attired damsels moved aside and sank into a variety of ungraceful curtseys, leaving the largest and plainest of them isolated in the centre.

For a moment the affianced pair gaped at each other. Then Anne essayed a wobbly curtsey.

'*Majesteit.*'

Henry's voice was completely flat, his mouth still slightly ajar.

'Welcome, Madam. Welcome to England.'

The princess had stuck halfway down in her curtsey and had an air of being marooned in a sea of ridiculous petticoat. Her face under the bright yellow hair was so pale that every mark on it stood out. Henry forced himself to approach her, to raise her and to aim a shrinking kiss on her brow.

'I trust Your Highness has not suffered from her journey.'

Anne gulped, willing the tears not to gather in her eyes. She had been told the King was an ageing man, that an accident had left him slightly lame, but she had not expected so gross a figure to appear before her without warning. He was enormous, she thought in terror, with shoulders padded into grotesque puffs and a monstrous stomach. But his face, with the small, tight mouth and the heavy-lidded slits of eyes, frightened her more. She had never known cruelty in her life but she sensed it now and sensed too that he was not pleased with her.

'*Ja, ja. Het was niet in onze verwachting Uwe Majesteit nu reeds te zien,*' she said breathlessly, her few carefully learned and prepared English sentences flying out of her head.

'Good.' Henry, who had obviously not understood a

word, bared his teeth in a ferocious smile.

Anne waved her hands towards her ladies, stammering slightly as she presented them.

'Sire, *geef orrlof dat ik U mijn edelvrouwen voorstel* —Baronesse Brempt, Gravin Osenbruch, Baronesse Loe, Vrouwe Willik, Vrouwe Swartzenbroch.'

Henry turned abruptly towards Cranmer who had ventured after him into the apartment and was now looking as if he wished himself back in his own See of Canterbury.

'Does she speak no other language except her own?' he asked incredulously.

'I will bring the interpreter, sir,' Cranmer offered.

'No, no, another time, my lord.' Henry gave the quaking princess a last displeased grin, and muttering, 'Your Highness. Good-day,' stalked out, his back a ramrod of indignation.

As the door closed behind them, Anne let out her breath in a little sigh. It had been worse, much worse, than she had expected. The King had not liked her. She had seen the coldly considering look in his eyes, heard the savage disappointment behind the words she couldn't understand.

Her ladies had gathered around her again and were chattering like magpies, exclaiming what a fine figure of a man she had found herself. But I didn't find him, Anne thought miserably. I was pushed at him like an unwanted meal and he obviously wanted to spit me out. Remembering the tight mouth and the narrow eyes she began to tremble again.

In the corridor Henry stamped towards Cromwell and Wriothesley, pulling Holbein's miniature from his breast as he came.

'Whom shall men trust in this world,' he choked, 'when there is nothing real in it! Is this a likeness?'

'Why, yes, sir——' Cromwell's jaw sagged slightly.

The King thrust the picture close to him, demanding, 'Then where are the great pits in her face? Eh?'

'Master Holbein may have taken some artistic licence,' Cromwell admitted.

'Some! *Some?* It is nothing like her. It is nothing like her at all!'

'I am sorry Your Grace is no better content,' Cromwell said sulkily.

'Content—to bed with that!'

'She has a queenly manner, I think,' his minister persisted.

'I'll give you a kingly one!' Henry exploded. 'I like her not.'

'Perhaps in time——'

Cromwell staggered slightly as Henry, purple with temper, beat his fists about his head and shoulders.

'I like her not!' he cried furiously. 'She is nothing like her portrait and nothing like she has been described to me by those whom I trusted. I am not well served.' His voice dropped in menace and he repeated, his eyes fixed upon Cromwell's sallow face, 'I am not well served.'

Wriothesley, seeing the King turn away, reminded him nervously, 'Your Grace has not yet presented the gift you brought.'

Henry's eyes fell upon the sables. He had chosen them personally and imagined their sleekness draped about the elegant form of the lady in the portrait. Upon this gracious image the figure of the woman he had just met intruded unpleasantly.

In a spasm of rage, he pulled the fur from Culpepper's hands and threw it towards Wriothesley.

'Give it to her yourself! For my own part I'm back to London, and you, Cromwell, will stir yourself!'

The echo of 'What remedy?' hung in the air when he had stormed out.

'But there is no remedy this time,' Cromwell said. 'The lady's character, her antecedents, all have been too carefully checked.'

'She was betrothed to Francis of Lorraine,' Wriothesley said hopefully.

'There is no impediment there,' Cranmer said gloomily. 'That arrangement was a purely formal one, entered into when both parties were children, and later formally annulled. The papers are still lodged in Cleves but copies were offered to us when we made enquiries.'

'The King may change his mind,' Wriothesley began, but Cromwell cut him short.

'Not from loathing to liking. Where His Grace has loved he may grow to hate, but he has never learned to advance in the other direction.'

Cranmer nodded while the thought crossed his mind that the speaker might do well to apply the lesson to himself. There were so many—Katherine, Nan Bullen, Thomas More, Bishop Fisher—whom the King had once loved and who had met their deaths by his orders. Cromwell, thought the Archbishop uneasily, had best beware, remember that it was he who had arranged this marriage and cease airing his knowledge of the King's opinions.

As for the poor princess—Cranmer glanced towards the closed door and sighed. Anne of Cleves seemed to be such a pleasant lady—but then, all His Grace's wives had been pleasant ladies.

The official meeting between the King and his bride took place on Blackheath and was as carefully rehearsed and as artificial as a play. The crowds watching the ceremonial embrace of Henry and Anne were too impressed by the splendour of their diamonds to notice their monarch's fixed and over-hearty smile or the nervous pucker of the bride's mouth as she tried frantically to pronounce words of greeting in an unfamiliar tongue.

At least the people like me, Anne comforted herself,

smiling from side to side as she mounted her horse. I wonder if they liked the other queens. That old man over there looks as if he would be able to remember Queen Katherine. I wish I could stop and ask him if she was pretty when she was young. They say that after death her heart was opened up and a black thing clung to the core of it. Don't think of that! Of what then shall I think? Of Anne Bullen's head falling upon the scaffold? Of Queen Jane Seymour laid among lilies so that her child should live? Better not to think at all, but to smile and bow my head and try not to notice the coldness in my bridegroom's eyes.

Henry, glancing at her, thought with savage mockery, She is decked out like a hobby-horse and resembles nothing so much as a great mare. And I must put my neck into the yoke with that! My other wives had dignity, beauty, and gentleness in their turn, but this fat Fleming has nothing to commend her. Yet if I send her home unwed her brother will run to join the Emperor. So I must sacrifice myself for the good of the country. One fact alone gives me comfort. This simpering fool with whom I can only converse through an interpreter is too stupid to recognise the revulsion on my face.

He raised a jewelled glove in the direction of the Duke of Norfolk who sat his horse with the same grace that had distinguished him when, as young Howard, he had thrown down the blood-stained mantle of the Scottish King. He was older now, of course, lean and spare, unlike Suffolk who had put on weight since he had taken another wife. She was a lovely, dark-eyed slip of a thing, Katharine Willoughby. Daughter to that lady-in-waiting, Maria de Salinas. There was another girl with Norfolk too. A tiny girl in a white dress with auburn hair like a flame about her head. Another of the tribe of Howard nieces, Henry supposed.

He grunted as Culpepper and another gentleman

eased him to the ground. Although hard ice packed the gutters and the wind was keen his face shone with sweat, and heat seared his leg in wave after wave of pain. He bared his teeth, cursing under his breath, and the fat Fleming giggled suddenly on a high, neighing note.

The dawn of the King's fourth wedding day was rain-spotted and mist-heavy; fitting omen, whispered the courtiers, for a marriage that seemed doomed from the start.

Henry had decreed that the service was to take place at eight o'clock, with some vague idea that after a day's feasting the prospect of a night alone with his new wife might not seem so daunting.

'At least I go to my marriage well-decked for sacrifice,' he told Culpepper, who tilted the mirror so that Henry could examine his reflection on its shining surface. The square-shouldered, full-bellied figure tapered to foreshortened legs and a glimpse of buckled shoe in a medley of gold and silver, crimson and black.

'Your Grace is trimmed for sail,' Culpepper ventured.

'Aye, Tom! But with what a cargo! And where is she, bye the bye? It is past eight already.'

Henry glanced impatiently at the clock.

'The Earl of Essex was to attend her but he's not yet come, sir,' an usher interposed.

'Then send Cromwell. It will give him something useful to do. It is a bad beginning when one is kept waiting by the bride!' Henry snapped.

And it was, he decided, not worth a minute's delay, for when he finally beheld his bride she was as lumpy and pock-marked as ever, despite her gown of cloth-of-gold and the rosemary twined in that long, thick, incredibly yellow hair.

He took her hand with distaste, noting that it was clammy with sweat. Essex had arrived after all and no doubt had remembered the ring with its inscription, 'God send me well to keep.'

And God help me speedily to be rid of her, Henry thought, darting a venomous glance towards Cromwell, who stood at one side looking so insufferably complacent that his master's fists involuntarily clenched and Anne gave a little whimper as her fingers were tightly squeezed.

She had been awake most of the night and her eyes were heavy from lack of sleep and unshed tears. It was all far, far worse than she had ever expected, and had it not been for the importance of the Protestant League she would have run straight home to Cleves.

Her brother had impressed upon her that England's support was vital to the Lutheran states. Without it they would have to turn to Catholic France and the Emperor. It was necessary for Anne to marry, but she wished with all her heart that it had been Sophia who had taken the King's fancy. But then Master Holbein had not painted so flattering a portrait of Sophia.

The unfamiliar service dragged on in a strange tongue. The ring was cold and heavy on her finger. She tried to follow the proceedings but her head ached and there was a smile fixed on her mouth as if her lips had been stitched into a permanent curve.

Later they sat under canopies, eating and drinking, while musicians played and girls, who were more beautiful than Anne could ever hope to be, danced before the high tables. Tudor roses and the white swans of Cleves decorated the jellies and sugar cakes.

And I, thought Anne, am like a swan, graceful when I bend over my spinning or kneel, trowel in hand, to weed my herb garden; for in those places I am in my right element. Here I am a swan on land, clumsy and comic.

Her eyes brimmed suddenly with tears and to hide them she bent her head and dug her spoon into the quince pie on her dish.

'The mare is tucking into her oats,' Henry muttered gloomily into Culpepper's ear, but gave no answering smile to the young man's impudent snort of laughter.

Much later, and yet sooner than Anne wished, they went in solemn procession up to the great bedchamber which she had glimpsed briefly through a half-open door earlier in the day.

Her ladies, whispering and giggling, escorted her into the curtained alcove where her nightclothes were laid across a chair. She had known these companions for many years but now she felt separate from them as if her body were moving forward to an experience for which her heart was not prepared.

Henry listened to the subdued chatter as he was divested of his own robes by the fire. Pages were making the sign of the cross over the silken pillows. Culpepper was still looking faintly amused. His master cuffed him none too lightly on the side of the head and scowled as fragments of guttural conversation drifted from behind the curtain.

'Zal Uwe Hoogheid dit dragen.'

'Of dit?'

'Ach, hoe schoon verschijn Uwe Hoogheid in deze tooi.'

'De koning wacht.'

'I promise you one thing,' Henry said, pulling his night-shirt over his head and emerging, tousled, to glare at the Duke of Suffolk. 'She shall have our own ladies and not those strange maidens who "moo" about her. They shall be shipped back to Cleves in the morning.'

'Yes, Your Grace.' Secure in the possession of a charming young wife, the Duke bowed solemnly.

The mooing maidens were emerging now from behind the curtain, bobbing to the ground and modestly averting their eyes from the nightshirted King. The last of them carried a cushion on which a flaxen wig rested. Henry's expression changed to the liveliest alarm, and Culpepper bit his lip to keep from grinning.

The curtains parted and Anne, her own dark hair about her shoulders, stepped out, clutching her nightgown around her plumply uncorseted figure.

'Good God, Madam,' was all that Henry could find to say as he gaped at her.

Anne smiled nervously, and having begun smiling found it impossible to stop; but went on foolishly stretching her mouth while perspiration rolled down her broad cheekbones and her breath came in little sobbing gasps.

'I wish Your Grace a pleasant good night,' Suffolk murmured, pulling at his beard and jerking his head towards the door as a signal for the others to leave.

They filed out in an embarrassed silence as husband and wife continued to stare at each other. In Henry's mind his other wives mocked this farce of a bedding. Katherine of Aragon turned up her haughty Spanish nose. Nan Bullen sneered, red-lipped and avid-eyed. Jane—but Jane was dead. Little, gentle Jane was dead, and this shapeless bundle of Flemish stupidity was alive. The unfairness of Heaven shook him into a gust of anger almost as strong as physical desire and Anne took a pace backwards, her eyes widening with dismay.

'Do get into bed, Madam,' Henry said impatiently, indicating the carefully blessed pillows and wondering wildly if it might not be possible to call the interpreter.

For so large a woman she fairly scuttled between the sheets. He occupied himself in blowing out the tapers, lingering at each one as if he were holding a silent conversation with it. Perhaps, in the darkness, she would be soft and yielding. But even then, beneath the covers, his hands groped over drooping breasts and sagging belly, and before the act was begun he had turned away and sunk into a dream of a white-clad girl with hair red as flame and a mouth ripe for mischief.

CHAPTER ELEVEN

The King and the Duke of Norfolk sat together beneath the canopy of the royal barge, Henry's bulk occupying most of the space on the cushioned bench. At his side, lean and neat, the Duke listened to His Grace's tirade, hooded lids drooping, hands wrapped within his fur-trimmed robe, an expression of deep sympathy on his narrow face.

'I can't touch her, Howard,' the King said miserably. 'All I say to her is goodnight and good morning, and she is so ignorant that she probably imagines that is all there is to a marriage. Yet they say she is admired in her own country.'

'In Cleves,' Norfolk said, 'the standards are surely lower than those to which we are accustomed, not to mention Your Grace's own fastidious taste.'

'Exactly so!' Henry nodded energetically.

'It is a sad irony,' the Duke reflected, 'that Your Grace wields supreme power and yet in areas of personal happiness is constrained.'

'Poor men may choose their wives,' Henry agreed. 'The meanest peasant can take a lovely girl, but I am saddled with a great Flanders mare.'

'Is it possible you might grow accustomed to her?' Norfolk enquired.

'I like her worse now than I did in the beginning,' Henry asserted. 'Someone, Cromwell no doubt, has told her to make herself more agreeable. She smiles at me. Indeed she never stops smiling at me. From morn till night she is perpetually smiling. It's enough to make a man run mad, and yet Cromwell keeps informing me that she is a fine figure of a woman.'

'Cromwell has much to gain, Your Grace,' Norfolk said.

His voice was low but clear beneath the swishing of the oars, and Henry bent closer to catch the words.

'I understand, from certain sources, that he received a pretty little sum from the Duke of Cleves when he arranged the marriage.'

'Well, it shall not be consummated,' Henry said sharply. 'Cromwell cannot arrange that for all his cleverness. A pretty sum, you say?'

'Very pretty, I believe. Of course, a man expects to be paid, I suppose, for services rendered.'

'And I expect my ministers to render service to *me*,' Henry frowned.

'Then what is to be done? Your Grace is in a coil it seems to me.'

'Coils can be unravelled. I'll find some means of annulling the marriage.'

'Your Grace shares the same sleeping quarters,' Norfolk hinted.

'That will be altered,' Henry said grimly. 'I'm packing her off to Richmond tomorrow for the sake of her health. There is a dower house there that belonged to the late Princess Dowager. The Queen may occupy herself quite happily with her spinning and weaving.'

'She does not sound the most exciting of companions,' Norfolk sympathised.

'The only thing that's pleasant in her company,' Henry said, 'is that little maid-in-waiting, your niece.'

'I have so many nieces.'

The Duke spread his fingers wide and regarded them indifferently. Then he spoke briskly, with the air of one concluding a discussion.

'But Your Grace ought not to trouble himself with these matters further today. We are all in sympathy with you, sir, and I for one am angered that your personal happiness should be endangered by ambitious men. Now you shall think on it no more for the present, but enjoy the fine supper my Lord Gardiner has prepared.'

'Yes, I like Lambeth.' Henry's eyes brightened. 'I like Gardiner's table. At my time of life a man begins to value good food and good fellowship.'

And the Bishop really set an excellent table, Henry thought later as he tucked into roast goose with caper sauce, pulling the joint between his fingers and spattering the rich gravy.

On one side of him Norfolk's fingers toyed with the stem of a wineglass as tenderly as if it were a lady's neck. On the other side Gardiner belched softly, patting his lips with a napkin.

Henry felt pleasantly full but not in the least sleepy. The excellent malmsey had stimulated him, making bright colours brighter, voices more pleasant. He listened to one voice in particular, higher and sweeter than the rest, with a lilt at the end of each sentence as if laughter bubbled out with the words. The owner of the voice sat further down the table, her small hands manipulating a silver fruit knife with such grace that Henry's eyes lingered with delight.

'Your little niece,' he said abruptly, 'is she a good girl?'

'Katheryn? Indeed, yes.' Norfolk gave her a casual, hooded glance. 'Her conduct is irreproachable, sir. Of the most pure and honest condition.'

'Not like another of your clan?' Henry asked.

'The Bullen?' Norfolk pronounced the forbidden name almost with indifference, and accompanied it with a snort. 'No, Your Grace! She is a good Catholic.'

'But orphaned, you said?'

'Her father, Edmund, was my youngest brother. After his death I did what I could for his children, but there were so many of them and my own resources are not limitless. The poor child has only her gentleness to commend her.'

'We will make her a grant of land,' Henry decided.

'She could not expect such a gift!' Norfolk exclaimed. 'She will say she has done nothing to deserve it.'

'She pleases me,' Henry said absently.

His eyes had flickered down the table again and his hands moved slowly, dismembering the remains of the goose in imitation of daintiness.

'The evening is so warm and light that Your Grace might care to take a stroll in the garden before returning to Westminster,' Gardiner suggested.

'Your niece can serve me as a guide.' Henry nodded affably at the Duke.

'She is very shy, scarcely out of the nursery,' Norfolk began.

'She is past seventeen, isn't she?' Gardiner interposed. 'For my own part I think her a charming girl. It is pleasant to meet a young lady who minds her manners in the presence of her elders and doesn't push herself forward.'

'If Your Grace feels she can amuse you——'

Norfolk beckoned to his niece who rose at once and came obediently to his side. Her childish mouth was faintly sticky with pear juice, and her lashes made curving crescents above her cheekbones.

'We have a fancy to walk in my Lord Bishop's garden before returning to Westminster,' Henry said. 'You will show me the beauties of the place if you'll be so kind, for I believe you know it well.'

He had spoken too formally, too abruptly, for the colour rushed into her small face.

'I was reared in Lambeth, Your Grace,' she answered shyly.

'By the Dowager Duchess, I understand.'

'She is my step-grandam, sir. She had always—done her duty by me.'

Katheryn's eyes sparkled suddenly as if they held tears. Henry had an impulse to put his arm round her, to protect her from whatever unhappy memory troubled her young thoughts.

As they strolled into the long evening shadows he took her hand, feeling it rest like a bird in his own great palm. She was so tiny that her head didn't even reach to his shoulder and her skirts rustled over the grass as if she had been fashioned from cobwebs and whispers.

'Your uncle tells me that you are a good girl,' he said, paternally, as if he spoke to a child.

'My uncle Norfolk is very kind. I have had much kindness, sir, for after my parents died I was quite alone, and my father's relatives took me in though they were under no obligation. And my Howard cousins give me their cast-off dresses, so I am most fortunate.'

An angel in cast-off gowns who counted herself 'most fortunate' because her relatives showed charity to her! Such a wealth of pity and tenderness overcame him that he ached with it.

'I have told your uncle Norfolk that I intend settling a grant of land on you,' he told her.

'Land? On me? But there is no reason—I have rendered no service!'

'Sometimes it pleases me to make gifts out of pure affection,' he told her, watching her troubled face. 'May not a man make a present to a girl young enough to be his daughter?'

The troubled expression vanished in a ripple of laughter.

'Sire, if that were true you must have been a forward child, for surely you are only just in your prime!'

At that moment, with the trees lacing their green leaves above, and a last gleam of sunlight gilding the water where the royal craft bobbed at anchor, Henry believed the statement to be true. With a little shock of pleasure he realised that his head had not ached nor his leg pained him for hours.

'And you will accept the gift?'

'Most gratefully, sir!' Katheryn gave a little skip as if she were still a child. 'I have always dreamed,' she said, a trifle breathlessly, 'of owning a small house in the middle of a garden.'

'And of living there alone like the princess in the fairy tale?' he teased. 'The Court cannot spare such beauty and such breeding as yours.'

'Breeding?' She looked up at him doubtfully.

'Never forget that you are a Howard,' Henry admonished kindly. 'The blood of kings runs in your veins, too, for we are both descended from Geoffrey of Anjou who founded the Plantagenet line.'

At a short distance the Bishop and the Duke stood together, their eyes following the slowly pacing couple, their voices discreetly low, for even in a garden there might be listening ears.

'A young wilding,' Norfolk mused, 'to whip the stale blood and lead him back to Rome—but how to do it, eh, my lord?'

'I believe if the matter were referred to the clergy at Convocation, that His Grace had wedded against his will——'

'And that it would prevent the threatened invasion. But the Queen would never agree to a divorce.'

'Annulment, surely,' the Bishop objected. 'As I understand it the marriage has not been consummated.'

'The lady may swear that it has,' Norfolk said gloomily.

'Who knows, if the terms were made sufficiently attractive she might even consent to become the King's adopted sister,' Gardiner smiled.

'And if she does not, we could always remind her of his other wives,' Norfolk finished.

'There's Cromwell to consider,' Gardiner warned.

The Duke's lips were scimitar-thin. 'He's abused his betters long enough. Katheryn will help us to get rid of him.'

'Is she obedient?'

'As a doe. No need to fret, my lord. My niece has lived too long on the scraps of charity to disdain a feast when it is spread before her. And she is an enchanting creature!'

Katheryn pattered up, matching her steps to the King's as she cried, 'But I never knew anything of this, Your Grace!'

'They have never allowed you to know your value,' Henry was saying. 'Not only are you Plantagenet, my dear, but you are also descended from Charlemagne. The College of Arms looked it up for me.'

'Does Your Grace approve of my garden?' the Bishop asked.

'And of the flowers in it.' Henry gave Katheryn a quick, shy smile that made him look like a reflection of his own splendid youth. 'I will bid you goodnight, Mistress'—he said, regret dragging the words—'Howard, for the present. A fine supper, Gardiner.'

The barge was waiting. Henry gave Katheryn a last smile and walked out on to the landing stage where his gentlemen were ready to help him aboard.

'You are greatly honoured, niece,' the Duke said in a low voice.

Trouble had rushed back into her vivid face.

'I had not looked for it, sir,' she faltered slightly. 'I had wished——'

'Mistress, you must no longer consider your own wishes,' Gardiner said sternly. 'You have a duty now to return England to the true faith.'

'And the King is most generous to those whom he loves,' her uncle reminded her. 'You like pretty clothes and jewels, don't you?'

'Yes, sir.' But she spoke doubtfully, twisting her hands together.

'We should go in,' Gardiner said. 'The grass is damp at this time of day, and it would be most unfortunate if you were to catch a chill.'

'We have your best interests at heart,' Norfolk assured her.

Katheryn nodded, smiling, and walked between them across the sloping lawn, but as she went she made a little fluttering gesture with her hands, like the last, desperate struggle of some condemned butterfly.

'His Grace has your best interests at heart,' the interpreter assured the Queen. 'In the plague months it is better for you to be at Richmond.'

She had to admit that the dower house was attractive and comfortable. There were pleasant gardens where she had already begun to plant fresh herbs and the view across the river was superb. In England she had more privacy than she had ever had in her life before, and even a little authority, for the servants came to her for orders regarding the food to be served and the tasks to be done. She had begun to work hard at her English lessons so that she could converse with people a little, and in the long, quiet evenings her ladies taught her card games.

Life, Anne considered, would be most enjoyable if only she were not married to the King. His physical appearance revolted her, for like many plain women she set high standards for masculine beauty and Henry's gross frame, the greedy eyes and tight mouth displeased her. But worse than that was the foetid stink that issued from his leg, and the sour-sweet breath that made her want to turn her face away when he kissed her good-morning. That he never attempted any deeper intimacies was a fact for which she thanked

God with the most heartfelt gratitude.

Yet he had been young and handsome once when he married his first bride. Katherine of Aragon had lived at Richmond for a time after the death of her boy-husband, Prince Arthur, and there were a few mementoes of her stay in the form of half-a-dozen little account books, an unfinished piece of tapestry, a mantilla bundled into an old chest and forgotten.

Sad Spanish princess, burdened with so many dead babies! But she had loved Henry, and he had loved her too once, for all that he had cast her off. When she reached that thought Anne began to tremble, because Henry had loved three wives and caused their deaths, so what hope could there possibly be for a wife whom he disliked?

The idea that she might be taken from the mellow brick walls of the dower house to the gaunt, dark Tower lay heavily across her mind. She tried to explain her fears to Cromwell when he came to visit her, but her command of the language was too slight and he merely smiled and nodded in a way that made it clear that he didn't understand, and she was too nervous to call the interpreter.

Instead she went back to her herb garden and her spinning, lifting her head sometimes to watch the river, dreading to see the royal barge sail round the bend. The King, however, was occupied with a new interest, it seemed.

'A very pretty little thing, Madam.'

'Cousin to Queen Nan Bullen, but younger and gentler. They say she dines with His Grace every day.'

'But she is a virtuous girl and will not become his mistress.'

Anne's ladies clucked and gossiped while their mistress listened, her expression serene, her heart thumping beneath her leather corset.

In the suite of rooms reserved for her use, Katheryn Howard pirouetted up and down, her skirts held high, her red hair tumbled about her neck, her green eyes wide with dreams of jewels and pretty dresses.

'I shall be Queen,' she whispered to her reflection in the glass.

And the face of the glass sparkled merrily even though, without warning, tears ran down her cheeks, which was quite ridiculous. Surely she, of all girls in the world, had least reason to weep.

In the corridor beyond the Council Chamber at Westminster, Bishop Gardiner stood with Cromwell in the angle formed by window and wall and nodded agreement to his companion's remarks. Both gentlemen had recently put on a little weight and looked like sleek, well-fed cats with ears pricked and claws sheathed.

The King, emerging from the Council Chamber and advancing down the corridor towards them, cocked a reddish eyebrow in friendly fashion. He looked, indeed, remarkably good-humoured for a man who no longer dwelt with his wife and whose latest fancy was virtuous.

'Your Grace.'

Bishop and minister bowed almost in unison as if to emphasise their concord.

Henry paused, one hand stroking his beard, his eyes alert and amused.

'Good-day, Cromwell—I hear you've been entertaining.'

'Oh, His Lordship gave me very great comfort at his house,' Gardiner smiled. 'A well-appointed dinner, luxurious apartments, a splendid array of gold plate.'

'Cromwell has developed excellent taste in furnishings,' Henry nodded.

'If Your Grace will excuse me.' The Bishop inclined his head, still smiling. 'I'll take my seat in the Chamber. I am now at the age when I need to be settled comfortably before I give my mind to discussion.'

'By all means,' Henry waved the prelate away and took Cromwell's sleeve, drawing him aside deeper into the recess as various members of the Council began to stream past down the corridor.

'We are pleased to see this amity,' Henry said. 'It is never easy for a monarch when his advisers quarrel.'

'Gardiner and I opened our hearts to each other at that dinner, sir,' Cromwell said earnestly. 'We pledged that for the sake of the realm, and for the sake of the love we bear Your Grace, all displeasure between us should be forgotten.'

'A profitable meeting.' Henry clapped the other upon the shoulder. 'You have also visited the Queen, I understand. How is she?'

'Very well indeed, Your Grace,' Cromwell answered eagerly, his voice hopeful. 'She is progressing with her lessons in English, and she is vastly improved in looks. You would be most surprised, sir, if you were to see her now.'

'Since the air of Richmond suits her so admirably we'll leave her there for the present. One thing more.' The King's voice was mellow but his lips had thinned slightly. 'What's this I hear about your land enquiry?'

'Sir?'

'Of the German princes—as to whether they have any lands or castles for sale.'

'Your Grace knows how rumours fly,' Cromwell said easily, tongue flicking his lips. 'Let one woman have a dizzy spell in the market place and within an hour folk are running from the plague.'

'Rumour? No more than that?'

'No, sir.'

Legs apart, the minister outstared the monarch.

'We should be sorry to think you were deserting us, especially for such Lutheran ground,' Henry teased.

'Indeed, sir——' Cromwell broke off as the Duke of Norfolk came towards them.

'Ah, Howard!' The King took a pace forward. 'Did you look at those yearlings for me?'

'Short-winded, Your Grace.' Norfolk curled his long upper lip. 'I sent them back with their tails cropped.'

'That's my Norfolk—a fine judge of horses; and women!' Henry exclaimed.

'Only of horses now, alas! We do not all possess Your Grace's stamina.'

Glancing at Cromwell, Norfolk insinuated himself into a bow and passed on into the Council Chamber.

'What were we talking about?' Henry enquired. 'Loyalty or some such thing, wasn't it?'

'Your Grace knows that I would never exceed the limits imposed by his Articles,' Cromwell said earnestly.

'And a Protestant Queen does not denote a Protestant country, does it? We are still Defender of the Faith, are we not?' Henry enquired.

'Indeed, yes, sir.'

'We would not care to deviate so far from Catholic doctrine. But we are delighted you are not going to Germany, that you remain here to do us such good service.'

'Sir, if I could——'

Cromwell hunched his shoulder impatiently as Wriothesley went past, his lean frame inclining towards the King.

'Your Grace.' The Secretary's voice was respectful, his eyes lowered.

'Good-day to you, Master Wriothesley.' Cromwell's voice, pitched a shade too loud, reproached his inferior and demanded attention.

Wriothesley's eyelids flickered faintly as he bowed.

'My Lord,' he murmured.

'You were saying——?' Henry turned again to

Cromwell.

'If it lies within my power to make Your Majesty still more prosperous——'

'But how could I ever reward you?' Henry joked. 'You already have it all—Vicar General, the Garter, the Earldom of Essex, and now Lord Chamberlain—what more could I do for you?'

'Your Grace might box my ears sometimes,' Cromwell suggested.

'Aha, that would no longer be fitting!' Henry chuckled as if something amused him immensely, and then sobered abruptly. 'But I am keeping Your Lordship from his business.'

The King gave his minister a friendly push and stalked away without a backward look.

Cromwell stared after him with a slightly puzzled frown before turning on his heel and walking with conscious dignity towards the Council Chamber.

At the threshold he paused, waiting for the perceptible hush that always greeted his arrival, but Edward Seymour had evidently not noticed him for his nasal voice rose above the chatter.

'My Lords, if we may have some order we can begin the day's business.'

The buzz of conversation died and Seymour pitched his tone a shadow lower as he continued, rather in the manner of a schoolteacher rebuking an unruly class.

'Now, my Lords, concerning the validity of His Grace's present union, and the Queen's precontract with the Marquis of Lorraine——'

'I thought that had been disclaimed,' interrupted Suffolk.

Cromwell, scowling displeasure, spoke sharply as he moved to his usual seat.

'You were in a great hurry, gentlemen, to begin without me.'

Seymour had resumed his speech, however, without

even a glance.

'Naturally Her Highness would need to remain in England as security for Cleves behaviour——'

He was interrupted again, this time by Norfolk, who half-rose in his chair, shouting across the width of the table.

'Cromwell. Do not sit there. It's no place for you. *Traitors* do not sit with gentlemen!'

Cromwell had stopped short, his shoulders hunched, his head lowered. The doors at the further end of the room opened in response to Norfolk's bellow and the halberdiers marched in to stand at each side of the King's most powerful Minister.

'My Lord of Essex, I arrest you in the King's name.'

Ignoring the Captain of the Guard, Cromwell thrust out his head to his old enemy, Norfolk.

'I am no traitor!' he cried. 'On your conscience, am I a traitor? Let me speak to the King.'

Norfolk had risen, his voice scratching the words as a fingernail rasps across silk.

'No, Cromwell. By your own law that no man accused of treason may attend His Grace. Take him, and you, Master Wriothesley, send to his house to make inventory.'

It was Suffolk who left his place, commanding the arresting officers to wait, stepping up to Cromwell and tearing from his neck the Order of St. George.

As he held it aloft, Norfolk joined him, his jewelled hands snatching like talons for the Order of the Garter, while around the table, the other lords crashed down their fists, chanting the word Cromwell himself had used so often of others.

'Traitor! Traitor! Traitor!'

THE TIME OF THE ROSE

❉❉❉

CHAPTER TWELVE

It was the season of delight, the golden autumn of a youth reborn. Every day was a pearl on a chain, a petal on a flower, and, when he held his new Queen in his arms, Henry knew quite certainly that winter would never come again.

Katheryn was so beautiful, her red hair loosely curling over her white shoulders, her green eyes tilting at the corners, her small nose faintly scattered with freckles as a rose carries a scattering of pollen at its heart.

Henry liked to watch her when she was not aware of it, to trace with his eye the tender curve of her neck as she bent over her lute, to wait for the moment when her eyes would meet his and her face would dimple into laughter.

It was even a part of their loving that from time to time he should pretend to be angry with her.

'Furs, velvets, sarcenets——' he grumbled now, looking at the swathes of material flung across the bed.

'You wanted me to have them,' Katheryn pouted.

'But not in such quantities, my darling. The treasury is not inexhaustible,' he protested. 'If it were we could have given you a public ceremony at St. Paul's.'

'Forgive me, do, forgive me!'

She was all pretty contrition now, her arms wound about his neck, and her eyes big with pleading.

'You know I can never refuse you anything,' he said, ruefully tender, for he could never bear even the pretence of displeasure for very long.

'You are the most generous of lords and I am the most fortunate of ladies,' she murmured.

He pulled her closer, winding a ringlet about his finger, seeing the long lashes cast their shadow above the high cheekbones.

'You woke last night in your sleep,' he remembered. 'You cried out.'

'I was dreaming badly, sir,' she said, and quivered for an instant as if his remark had brought back the horror of nightmare.

'Of what?'

'There was a bird caught in the room,' she said slowly.

'In your dream?'

'Flying against the walls, the bed curtain, beating at the window. I went to free it but it was the devil in the shape of a bird.' Her voice shook with terror and there was a pinched look at the corners of her mouth. 'When I caught it, it cried out in the devil's voice before I broke its neck. "Blind, blind, hoodman blind, help me cousin or I——" it cried.'

She stopped, awareness creeping back into her eyes.

'It was but a dream, sir,' she whispered. 'Only a dream.'

'Do you remember your cousin?' he asked. 'The Bullen?'

'Sometimes,' she confessed. 'I saw her at her Coronation. She was clad all in gold and her hair was black. I thought her beautiful, sir.'

'I too made the same mistake,' Henry said sombrely, and his face was bitter. 'My only excuse is that I was younger then and dazzled by the black and the gold.'

'You are young still,' she began and paused as Lady Rochford appeared at the door. Henry had frowned slightly and loosened his hold upon the Queen.

He could not have said precisely why, but he disliked the lady-in-waiting intensely. One ought, he knew, to feel pity for a woman whose husband had committed incest with his own sister, but he could never forget how eagerly Lady Rochford had rushed forward with her tale. Yet Katheryn seemed to be very fond of her and the two of them were forever giggling in corners.

'Do you have him?' Katheryn demanded, jumping up.

'Have I Your Grace's permission?' Lady Rochford began.

The Queen, impatient of formality, cried out, 'Oh, bring him in.'

Lady Rochford hesitated, glancing doubtfully towards the King.

'Bring him in,' Katheryn repeated imperiously. 'Quickly!'

The lady-in-waiting gave a small shrug as she went out, as if to disclaim responsibility, and returned a moment later with a small puppy. She placed it gingerly on the floor, where it proceeded to scamper, uttering shrill barks of ecstasy.

'Not another one!' Henry exclaimed, staring at the animal in consternation.

Katheryn was on her knees with hands held out coaxingly to the little dog.

'He's delightful! Look at him trying to wag his tail. Isn't he sweet?'

'But you have three already, Madam,' Henry exploded.

Katheryn, abandoning the attempt to wean the puppy from its newly-discovered liberty, returned to her husband's side, slipping her arm through his and twinkling up into his face.

'He is not for me,' she confided. 'He is for the Lady Anne.'

'Of Cleves?'

'She was always so kind to me,' Katheryn wheedled. 'I liked her very much even if she was too fat and couldn't speak any English. And she sent me a gift on our wedding day. So I thought you wouldn't mind too greatly if I were to buy her something in return. Please allow me.'

'All the settlements I had to make on her,' he groaned. 'The income, the manors, the estates—and now a spaniel!'

'But she would so like to have the little dog,' Katheryn begged. 'May I give it to her? *Please.*'

The King looked briefly and feelingly up to the ceiling as if he were consulting an ally, and then nodded.

'If you must,' he said heavily.

'Now you are cross with me,' Katheryn said sulkily. 'I wanted to do the Lady Anne a little kindness, and you are cross with me.'

Her face had crumpled and tears beaded her long lashes. Lady Rochford had tactfully withdrawn, with a look of amused sympathy which Henry had pretended not to see. The puppy, as if aware that it was the subject of discussion, had sat down on its haunches and was regarding them sorrowfully.

'I'm not angry; not in the least angry,' he said feebly. 'It's a very nice little thing. She can have it.'

'Your Grace is so kind,' Katheryn cried. 'Thank you. Oh, thank you, sir.'

Her face, bright again, her arms about Henry's neck. She was so slender that he could have snapped her like a twig, but even as he put up a hand to cup her breast she had danced away again, and catching up the dog, held it out to the young man who had strolled into the doorway.

'Master Culpepper!' Her voice was imperious again. 'Will you have this dog sent to my Lady of Cleves as quickly as possible?'

'Your Grace.' Culpepper bowed, taking the small creature with such distaste on his face that Henry burst out laughing.

'Have a care for your fine breeches, Thomas! Our

friend is not yet house-trained.'

'I'll come with you and see the poor little thing safe into a travelling basket,' Katheryn declared.

'Aye! Do that, for from the gleam in Tom's eye he may very well drop it accidentally into the moat on his way out,' Henry retorted.

He smiled to himself as he listened to their retreating footsteps punctuated by the shrill yapping of the puppy. Katheryn was little more than a child herself, for all the airs she assumed in front of Culpepper. The two of them made him feel young and lusty again. And it was kind of her to think of giving a present to the Lady Anne.

The Flanders mare was now 'sweet sister' to the husband who had never bedded her. Rubbing his leg, which had begun to ache a little, Henry reflected that the divorce had been managed most comfortably. It was true that Anne had panicked when the divorce petition was brought to her and had collapsed in a dead faint at Milord Suffolk's feet, but once revived with vinegar and a burnt feather she had agreed cheerfully that her precontract with the Marquis of Lorraine rendered her present union with King Henry invalid. She had been, Henry considered, almost deplorably cheerful about it. A lady with more sensitivity might have protested a little more.

Anne, however, had retired placidly, loaded with estates and beaming goodwill, and Katheryn and Henry had been married very quietly with no more than the simplest ceremony. Now, in late life, he was suddenly young again, trembling with desire when she entered the room, aching with a passion he was certain he had never felt before.

A few days later, he shook with passion of a different kind as he sat, his leg propped on a stool, listening to the words of his Council, several of whom attended him with bad tidings written all over them.

'The North was ever independent, Your Grace, and they have their own ideas on most subjects.'

'In Yorkshire they declare that the loss of revenue caused by the dissolution of the abbeys makes it impossible for them to pay the increased taxation.'

'And Parliament will not vote a farthing more. They wanted to negotiate a peace with France.'

The King's fist banged down upon the arm of his chair and his voice rang out more furiously than they had heard it for many weeks.

'I should have listened to Cranmer! He said the Earl was such a servant as no prince ever had, and he was right. Cromwell knew how to raise a levy. Cromwell knew how to prod Parliament into granting me the sun and the moon if I had desired them.'

'Cromwell,' said Norfolk unwisely, 'is dead.'

'Done to death by the vicious slanders of his enemies,' Henry glared. 'Arrested on light pretexts, condemned by false accusation—you made me put the man to death.'

'His Grace is not well,' Norfolk murmured, but the King caught the murmur, swelling it into a roar.

'Well enough to know when I have been cozened! Well enough to know that in Cromwell I had a loyal and efficient servant, but you, like wolves, must drag him down and tear him to pieces.'

'We were concerned only for Your Majesty's safety,' Gardiner placated.

'And for your own profit no doubt!' Henry turned bright, cold eyes towards the Duke of Norfolk, and spoke in a measured, menacing tone. 'I know the good servants from the flatterers, and if God lends me health, Howard, I will take care such projects do not succeed. Now leave me!'

They bowed with closed, set faces, jostling one another slightly in their eagerness to leave the royal presence. As Seymour closed the door with unnecessary gentleness, Henry shouted again impatiently and Tom Culpepper emerged at once from the inner chamber, carrying the ewer of warm water and clean bandages with which the King's ulcer must be dressed twice a day.

As he knelt to unwind the stinking, pus-soaked bandage, Henry spoke again, irritably as if to a backward child.

'Make sure it's open. Dr. Buttes says it must discharge easily, otherwise it brings on the fever.'

'Yes, Your Grace.' Culpepper's face was slightly averted.

The King, frowning a little, enquired abruptly, 'Does it offend you to have to do this?'

'No, sir.' Culpepper shook his head, sponging the dried blood gently.

'I don't wish the Queen to see it,' Henry said painfully. 'And there is nobody else I can trust.'

He looked down again at the bent, glossy head, and the skilful fingers.

'Are you honest, boy?'

'Your Grace?' Culpepper's face was tilted upwards now, with a wary, startled look on it.

'You have never shown me anything but loyalty and affection. *Ugh!*'

Henry groaned faintly as the young man's fingers clenched upon the bandage, dragging it across the open wound.

'You might have been my son,' he said after a moment.

'Your Grace does me too much honour,' Culpepper said formally.

His head was bent to his task again but his fingers trembled as they wound the bandage.

'Not too tight now,' Henry warned. 'It's strange that it should have begun to fester again when I was feeling so improved. Buttes thinks that the fistula was caused by that fall I took. Remember?'

'Yes, sir.'

'And not God's judgment.'

Henry looked about vaguely as if for reassurance.

'It was a most dangerous accident, sir,' Culpepper agreed. 'It might have cost you your life.'

'Well, I can't joust any more,' Henry conceded. 'But when this is healed I'll rise at five, hear Mass at seven, and ride until dinner time. And not eat so much.'

He looked wryly from his own paunch to Culpepper's hard, flat stomach outlined under the tight doublet. There had been a time when he too had been lean and muscular.

'You'll tire us all yet, sir,' Culpepper said cheerfully. 'Not a man in the kingdom works longer or harder than Your Grace—they know it, and love you for it.'

'Yet still they refuse, and rebel.'

The King brooded for a moment and then slapped down his palm upon his sound knee.

'The progress planned for next month,' he decided. 'We'll go upon it still, to receive the homage of our rebel subjects in Yorkshire. When they know their monarch is come among them they'll pay the levy fast enough. But there'll be hunting up north and game in plenty.'

'It sounds fine sport, Your Grace.'

'We will make it so. I am not so lame that I cannot mount a horse, nor so old that I cannot bring down a buck. Have you finished?' Henry's gave the young man a light buffet on the shoulder. 'Off with you then!'

When Culpepper had gone the King leaned back in the chair, staring gloomily at his padded, bandaged leg. The sight and the stench of it would revolt Katheryn, and the pain of it prevented him from making love to her as often as he wished. Yet she never reproached him for the nights he did not visit her. However, if there were to be a child, he must improve his health, lose some weight, persevere with the treatments urged upon him by the doctors. Privately he doubted if even Buttes knew for certain what had caused the fistula.

He must have fallen into a light doze, for though he was still aware of himself slumped in the chair he also seemed to be watching himself, as if a brightly coloured screen unrolled behind his eyes. He was on horseback there, riding down the lists, half-crouched in the stirrups with his visor unclosed and the lance poised delicately in his hand.

And then the lance shattered and the wall loomed up, rising out of the bare ground. There was pain in his head and a thousand splinters in his heart, and young Culpepper stood, with a terrified expression on his face while his boy's hands automatically soothed the nervous horses.

Thin hands, brown hands, like the hands of the girl in the page's suit. He had swung her up to the saddle and ridden with her through a town he couldn't remember on a day he couldn't recall. There had been a sweet, wild look about her mouth and eyes, and on her slim body the raised blemish of a strawberry.

The Bullen had been marked, too. He saw again the long neck with its wide, concealing band of velvet.

'Your task will be easy, sir, for I have but a little neck.'

Giggling merrily with her fingers to her throat. That was how she had died. Husky, gurgling sobs of mirth that shrilled up into hysteria so easily when she was crossed. Katherine had had a pretty laugh when she was young.

Odd how the laughter of women echoed in the air long after their deaths, long after voices were stilled, and their faces grown dim. The girl with the strawberry mark laughed again and then the wall blotted out the sky. The world was full of pain and his leg throbbed unbearably and his wife's laughter danced in and out of flashes of agony.

He was in his chair again, blinking down over his paunch to the swollen, bandaged limb propped up before him. From outside the open window he could hear Katheryn's laughter ringing up from the courtyard. He reached for his stick, heaving himself upright in preparation for the limping walk across the floor.

Katheryn and Tom Culpepper were below, playing with the little dog intended for Anne of Cleves. Once before Henry had stood above a courtyard and watched his Queen amuse herself with her pets. The Bullen had set her greyhounds to fight, urging them on with blood-lust in her narrow face. But there was a gaiety and an innocence in the two figures who tossed a ball of coloured thread for the puppy to chase.

Sunlight briefly gilded Culpepper's brown head and the Queen's straying auburn curls so that they looked as if they had been dipped in honey. Then Katheryn glanced up and blew a kiss and touched Culpepper on the arm. And they stood, faces upturned to the King, the spaniel jumping about their feet, and the sunshine all round them like a benediction.

'Her Grace is very pretty,' said a voice at the King's elbow.

'Very pretty indeed,' Henry agreed, turning to survey his younger daughter with unwonted amiability.

Elizabeth was, he conceded, a pretty child herself, tall for her age and combining the vivid colouring of the Tudors with the narrow bones of the Boleyns. He seldom looked at her, however, without feeling a slight distaste, as if behind the child's inexperienced features stirred the adult emotions of a subtle woman. Neither would he ever forgive her for not having been born a boy.

But the sweetness of Katheryn's presence had mellowed his own mood to such an extent that pride in his child overcame aversion.

'You are growing up, Elizabeth,' he said warmly, 'and your tutors tell me you are very clever for your age.'

'His Grace, Prince Edward, is very clever for his age too,' she said with a quick and charming generosity.

'Ah, well, he is a boy,' Henry said kindly. 'The brains of men are stronger than the brains of women.'

'Was not my great-grandam, the Lady Margaret, one of the cleverest people in England?' she enquired.

'She was an exception,' Henry said.

Elizabeth's face took on a faintly mulish expression as if she were preparing to make an exception of herself, too.

'The Queen is going to send the gift of a puppy to the Lady Anne,' Henry said.

'The Queen is always giving presents.'

Elizabeth craned her neck and waved her hand while a purely childlike expression of delight stole into her too-composed face.

'I liked the Lady Anne's looks, you know,' she remarked irrelevantly.

'Which shows your taste needs developing,' Henry muttered. 'You had a mother whose beauty compared with that of the Cleves princess was as the sun against the soil.'

The little girl gave him a swift, frightened look. It was the first time she could ever remember his mentioning the mother whose name was never spoken. Somewhere in her mind a thin-waisted figure in black swooped and swirled, but despite all her efforts she could never see the head.

'This Queen, sir,' she said, timidly, 'will stay for a long time, won't she?'

'You are fond of her, aren't you?' Henry was pleased.

Elizabeth nodded.

'Her Grace has given me leave to stay up for supper

tonight and to sit next to her,' she said eagerly. 'May I, sir?'

'Her Grace will spoil you.'

Henry pinched his daughter's cheek. A pity this one was a bastard like Mary. He had it in mind to legitimise one or both of them if there were no child of this new marriage.

Then he caught up his own thoughts and gave Elizabeth a little push towards the door. He and Katheryn had been married such a little while. There was plenty of time for she was still young and he must endeavour to improve his own health.

In the weeks that followed, it began to seem as if Henry could really push back time by the sheer exercise of his gigantic will. He dieted vigorously, reduced his consumption of wine, rose at five and was in the saddle at six. An illusion of youth brightened his features and his voice rang out almost as heartily as in the days he had called to his first Katherine, bidding her watch him excel in the dance.

Now another Katheryn hearkened to his words, welcomed him into her bed, lit into a smile when he entered the room. Now it was Henry who sat applauding while Katheryn twisted and turned in the steps of the latest dance, leaping high into the air with her skirts belling out while Tom Culpepper waited to catch her on his arm.

But often Katheryn would refuse to dance and, delighting Henry by her neglect of the younger gallants, would settle herself at his knee and play the lute for him, pouting when she missed a note and complaining that he made her forget her skills when he roused in her such amorous desire.

Yet between the sheets she was coy and trembling, like some delicate bird he had chanced to catch. She suffered greatly from headaches and there were many nights when, warned by the strain on her white face, he would kiss her goodnight at the threshold of her room and go back to his own apartments.

She ought, he decided, to have children of her own, for there was in her nature something to which children responded. Edward held out his arms whenever his pretty stepmother went to visit him, and Elizabeth forgot her precocious dignity and romped like the little girl she was.

It was a pity, Henry reflected ruefully, that Katheryn could not make herself more popular with some of the older members of the Court. It was not her fault that she had the tactlessness of youth or a light, sometimes careless way of speaking that made some of the staider gentlewomen look down their noses at her.

Once he tried to tell her gently that she must have some concern for their traditional notions, but Katheryn had flashed out like an angry little kitten.

'Let them mind their own manners and remember that I am the Queen!'

'But there was no need to speak so slightingly to Howard because he would not join in your game, darling,' Henry coaxed.

'My uncle Norfolk is an old man and his son is a popinjay,' Katheryn said indignantly.

'Howard is my oldest friend,' Henry began, but she flung her arms about his neck.

'He is too old, and that is the trouble, for he will have you in your dotage long before your time.'

'I am no longer young,' Henry said mildly, but she contradicted him as he had known she would, assuring him over and over that he was in the very prime of his manhood, and that in comparison with him, she was an old lady.

'For I *shall* be old one day,' she informed him gravely. 'My hair will be white, and my eyes dim, and I shall cup my hand to my ear when people speak to me. Will you love me then, sir?'

'Madam, I will always love you,' he said, and knew that it was quite beyond his power to imagine her as anything other than young.

CHAPTER THIRTEEN

The rebellion was over. The King, faced with the gratifying duty of receiving the submission of the northern lords, combined this task with the long-planned progress. It was the first time he had taken his new Queen about in public and half his joy lay in witnessing her own delight.

Katheryn was pleased with everything and everyone was charmed by the little, dainty consort who was so interested in the countryside through which they travelled, so grateful for the entertainments devised by citizens trying desperately to prove that they were loyal subjects who would never dream of refusing to pay a tax demanded by their King.

Even the charcoal-burners' hovels on the edge of the forests enchanted Katheryn. She pronounced them sweet and declared nothing would please her more than to live for ever in such rustic simplicity. Her face within the depths of an ermine hood was completely serious as she made the statement and her velvet-shod feet tapped impatiently as if they longed to trudge up and down some miry lane.

When Henry laughed at her notions she first waxed indignant and then admitted there was something to be said for warm clothes and rich food and a fine horse to ride.

Mounted on her favourite chestnut and wearing a new green riding habit, Katheryn was at her most sparkling as she waited with the other members of the hunt at the edge of the clearing. In the thick hedgerow, beaters were drumming out the deer, and the clashing of their metal shields vied with their harsh cries of warning.

Overhead thick, grey clouds threatened the last rays of pale sunlight that lingered in the green hollows, and far off a low rumble of thunder set the small forest creatures quivering.

A stag burst from the thicket and was pierced at once by a dozen darts, sinking beneath their weight in a slow, almost indolent fashion until the proud, antlered head lay heavy too, with glazing eyes and panting breath.

'The next one is mine! Let me take the first shot!' Katheryn cried.

She sat her mount elegantly with one slim leg hooked over the pommel, and her bow held tightly against her shoulder. Her eyes were as green as her habit and tendrils of red hair blew over her white forehead. A doe, large-eyed and spindle-legged, trotted from the shelter of the trees and paused, nostrils scenting death, near to the body of the fallen stag.

For an instant the forest seemed to hold its breath as the animal turned a puzzled, accusing gaze towards the group of riders bunched together near the twin oaks that guarded the entrance to the clearing. In this silence, doe and Queen looked at each other in an intent, feminine way. Then Katheryn drew her bow and the deer fell.

A cheer startled a flock of sparrows into the sky from which large drops of rain were spattering. Katheryn turned a flushed and smiling face towards the King and he, forgetting the gaping beaters and the applauding courtiers, spurred his mount towards her and, leaning from the saddle, embraced her openly.

Even as he did so a dull leaden flash parted the clouds and the rain poured down, turning the hard earth into a sea of mud, bending the branches under its weight of water. Leaving the beaters to drag away the slaughtered beasts, the Court raced for shelter.

Because of lack of accommodation in the village they had pitched tents beyond the woodland. Katheryn had cried out happily that now they could all live like gypsies, though surely no gypsy ever had such a luxurious pavilion as the royal tent with its thick carpets and portable furniture.

Within the tent, dripping and shivering, Henry turned to watch his wife, who stood at the entrance, half in and half out of the rain, her long hair tangled under the little feathered hood.

'Oh, I can kill them, and I can kill moles, and I can kill vermin that creepeth up and creepeth down and peepeth into holes,' she sang in her sweetly husky voice.

'Come here, you rat-catcher!' Henry growled, pulling her within the circle of his arm and kissing her wet face.

She leaned against him for a moment and then spoke curtly to someone who sat in the gloom further inside.

'You can go now.'

The man with a sword-scar puckering his cheek rose from the desk, folded the letter he had been writing, and went out with a little swaggering bow.

Henry became aware that Katheryn was shivering violently and began with clumsy tenderness to unfasten her cloak, scolding her for getting wet as he hunted about for towels and a dry robe.

'Who was that man?' he remembered to ask as he drew off his own surcoat.

'The new secretary, sir.'

'I've not seen him before, have I?' he said and tried to place the handsome, insolent face.

'He was in attendance on my grandmother,' Katheryn said.

Her voice was flat and dull as if her gaiety had drained out of her with the life blood of the deer.

'What is his name then?'

'Derham, sir.'

Her voice had the same dead quality and when Henry looked at her she was crouched on a low stool, her naked shoulders unprotected from her wet hair, the riding habit in a sodden mass about her thighs, and a bleak edge to her profile.

'Is something the matter?' he demanded.

'I'm cold,' she answered and flashed him her warm and brilliant smile.

He came over hastily to put a robe about her.

'We must not have you ill. You have looked pale lately.'

He had only just discovered the fact himself, seeing her loveliness now as something fragile, her sparkle as a brittle, spun-glass affair.

'No, sir, I am in good health,' she reassured him.

'Are you with child?' he asked hopefully, but she shook her head, veiling her eyes with her long lashes.

A brief flare of disappointment caused him to speak more roughly than he had intended.

'I had a special jewel made for you, Madam. I had hoped to have given it to you by now.'

Katheryn brightened at once, her eyes glowing.

'A jewel, sir?' she asked eagerly. 'Do you have it here? Will you show it to me?'

His irritation vanished for she was, after all, no more than a child, with a child's greed and shallow miseries.

'It was to have been a reward, Madam. I see now that it must be a pledge instead.'

She was gazing in rapture at the diamonds embedded in pearls and emeralds.

Henry enjoyed her pleasure for a moment and then turned over the jewel, tracing the writing engraved on the back.

'Do you like your motto?' he wanted to know.

'You know I read badly, sir,' she said innocently.

'The Rose Without a Thorn,' he spelled out.

'Is that me, sir?' The colour rose up in her face as she stared at him.

He nodded with a sudden constriction in his throat that made speech impossible though words bubbled in his brain.

The pomegranate is sucked dry and the white falcon is headless, the snowdrop is laid in the earth and the mare put out to pasture; but the rose blooms, smooth-stalked and velvet-petalled, red as blood and white as snow, shedding its sweetness drop by drop into the aridity of my old age.

'Take it, Katheryn,' he said at last. 'Wear it now for me.'

She was still staring at the valuable token with parted lips and shining eyes. In grateful humility that the living treasure should be his, Henry lowered himself on to his sound knee and pressed his face against her bare thigh, kissing over and over the dark mole on the white flesh.

'Oh, my love. My very little girl,' he murmured.

If he had chanced to look up at that moment he would have seen that there was nothing childish about the misery on her face.

The jewel appeared proudly, however, on the Queen's dress and was duly admired, though Katheryn herself seemed to droop a little in the last days of the progress, so that Henry was not as regretful as he had expected to be when they began the journey back to London.

Winter was setting in, anyway, and soon the roads would be almost impassible. His leg throbbed more acutely when there was snow on the way, and the bitter wind made his head ache.

He looked forward to the warmth of leaping fires, to tankards of hot spiced malmsey, to chestnuts popping in the red coals. Yuletide would be upon them soon, and for Katheryn there would be furs piled high so that she could sink into them.

It was on the day that he had ordered a Mass of Thanksgiving to be said for the happiness of his marriage that Cranmer slid into the seat beside him and, under cover of the chanting, thrust a narrow sheaf of papers into his hand.

A casual glance—that was all it took for the whole world to rock dangerously, and then he was angry, too angry to remember the exposed Host upon the altar, the courtiers kneeling around him, the reason for the service.

Those who saw him leave, with Cranmer stumbling after, said later that he had walked without a trace of a limp and that the glint in his eyes had been murderous.

At that moment, indeed, he hated the entire Court with a passion that was almost like love. But what did any of them know of love, of the tenderness that could spring up between a man and a girl? They were jealous of him, envious because in old age he had found the sweetest and strongest of his loves.

He would not, he vowed, scanning the malicious lies, allow them to diminish this joy that had come to him so late. He would disregard the matter entirely, for she was his rose without a thorn, and none should touch her petals.

At the next Council meeting he was at his spriteliest, voice hearty and resonant, face flushed and eyes alert. It gave him a secret pleasure to look from his daïs over the assembled Council as if he were God and they a choir of extremely incompetent archangels. They were also extremely nervous and subdued archangels, he thought with a glint of humour, noting Cranmer's strained expression and the way in which Norfolk constantly cracked his finger-joints.

'Well, my lords, shall we begin?' Henry brought the already silent company to silence.

It was Edward Seymour, according to formula, who rose to reply. Jane's brother looked grave and drawn as ever but there was a tenseness in his voice out of all proportion to the sense of his words.

'Your Grace, we wish to tender our congratulations upon your safe return, and we are pleased to learn that Your Grace's subjects in the North show such gratifying repentance.'

'And in such gratifying coin, my lord,' Henry added amiably.

Seymour gave a bleak, nervous little smile.

'Our return is also blessed with the return to health of the Prince,' Henry went on. 'We asked our holy father of Lincoln to draw up a thanksgiving for this and for our good life with the Queen.'

Out of the corner of his eye he saw Cranmer on his feet, heard the softly pedantic voice.

'Sir, it is upon that subject——'

'And know this, my Lord Archbishop, we will not have Her Grace subjected to malicious gossip.' Henry put up a hand, his cold eyes probing the faces of those before him. 'We will not have secret papers thrust into our hands. Nor will we believe such calumnies, coming as they do from Protestant members of this Council.'

Norfolk and Gardiner exchanged brief smiles. As representatives of the older aristocracy any slur against a Catholic Queen touched them too closely.

Cranmer took a step forward, cleared his throat, and began to speak slowly and reluctantly.

'Your Grace will have to know that since our first discoveries certain examinations have been conducted.'

'Gropings, d'ye mean? The rack?'

Into the King's mind came a picture of the mutilated Smeaton.

'No, sir, simple enquiries into Her Grace's childhood. Voluntary confessions made by the waiting-women in her grandmother's house.'

'And you believe servants' gossip?'

'Sir, their evidence is well substantiated, and can be confirmed by my Lord Admiral and the Duke of Suffolk.'

'You've been busy, haven't you?' Henry said lightly, contemptuously.

'Your Grace requested me to verify the facts,' Cranmer said without reproach.

'For our protection,' Henry snapped. 'To put a stop to these slanders. I eat larks, my lord, I don't listen to them.'

Cranmer made an ineffectual gesture with his hands, then tucking them again within his wide sleeves took his seat once more and looked towards the Duke of Suffolk who rose heavily.

'Your Grace, we have indeed talked with the gentlewomen who were in service to the Duchess of Norfolk,' he said. 'Several of them were privy to the Queen's guilt and can testify to the evil life led by Her Grace before her marriage to you.'

'I give it no credence,' Henry said. 'Suffolk, you have always been my friend. You married my youngest sister. Why do you repeat these lies now?' His words ran on silently beneath the assumed smile.

Suffolk planted his feet wider apart and continued stolidly.

'The lesser misconduct took place with one, Manox, a musician, when Her Grace was but thirteen years of age. The more culpable was a Master Derham.'

'Derham? A scar on his face——'

'Both these men were subsequently examined by Your Grace's secretary.'

As Suffolk sat down Wriothesley rose to his feet as if they were all engaged in some macabre game. The Secretary had an oily, unctuous manner which set

Henry's teeth on edge.

'Derham admits, sir, that he was accustomed to visit Her Grace's chamber at night, and that they exchanged many gifts and love-tokens.'

'Howard, you told me she was pure,' Henry accused in anguish. 'You said there was no impediment to her marriage.'

'The man Derham denies any familiarity with the Queen since her marriage, sir,' Wriothesley said.

'And this was some years ago?'

'Yes, Your Grace.'

'And she has always shown perfect love to me.'

Henry spoke the words almost pleadingly into the silence.

She was a child then, flattered by a smooth tongue and a handsome face. And she was lonely, without parents, brought up in a large, disorderly household with nobody to train her in the way she should go. But I have loved her and sheltered her as the wall protects the rose. She is grateful for that and out of her gratitude sprang her love. Must I forsake her now because she is a faulty human being and not the perfect creature my imagination had devised?

Cranmer leaned forward, hatefully persistent as was his way when he had screwed up his courage.

'Your Grace must consider the circumstances of Master Derham being lately taken into the Queen's service,' he said earnestly. 'It proves her intention to wrong Your Grace.'

'How so?'

'If Her Grace wished to forget her evil companions she would not have brought one of them into the Court. That she did so proves she craves still for her old habits, and is guilty of presumptive treason.'

They were talking nonsense of course. Presumptive treason indeed! How could those words be applied to a child?

'You spoke of another,' Henry said dry-mouthed. 'A man called Manox.'

'A musician, Your Grace,' Cranmer nodded. 'He was employed in the household of the Duchess of Norfolk, and dismissed by her.'

'He confesses, sir, to having felt the secrets and other parts of the Queen's body, to having seen a private mark on her person,' Wriothesley said.

The horror in his voice was spiced with an unpleasant relish. Henry wanted to scream at him to be quiet, but he could only sit, trapped above them all in the great chair, hearing each word like a separate hammer blow against the foundations of his world.

'Derham openly boasts that he has known Her Grace carnally many times, and that he has done so in the presence of these servants.'

So it had not been a matter of a few smiles, a few gifts. There had been movements in the half-dark, glimpses of white flesh in the half-light, the subtle murmurings from ear to ear that took the place of conversation. Pain twisted his heart as if someone were digging out the sinews with a knife.

He opened his mouth once or twice but only a few sobbing breaths escaped him. His hands moved gropingly up to his face, pressing there as if he sought to crush out of his skull the picture of his young wife in the arms of other men. He began to rock a little from side to side, cradling his own agony, and then sobs were torn from him and scalding tears obscured the uneasy, embarrassed faces of his Council.

One by one, led by Cranmer, they rose and made their way from the apartment until it was empty save for the grotesque, heaving figure of the King, and silent save for his weeping.

In the corridor, Cranmer drew an unsteady breath. 'It is a terrible thing to see a man wounded to death,' he said.

'The Queen is guilty,' Seymour said.

'But so young! So very young.'

'My sister was young too,' Seymour said. 'Jane was young and gentle, and died bearing his child. He swore then that he would never love again.'

'This was his last love,' the Archbishop said sadly.

'His last love?' Edward Seymour gave a cynical shake of the head.

'The King will divorce her. He will put her into a convent.' Cranmer spoke hopefully as if he were trying to convince himself.

'Can you imagine the beauteous Katheryn in a convent?' Suffolk, who had come up behind them, gave a snort. 'She would be climbing over the grilles before she had been there a day.'

'Then if it is not to be divorce?' Cranmer asked the question, his mild eyes fearful.

'Her Grace is confined to quarters while more investigations are conducted. I took that liberty myself lest Norfolk take it into his head to whisk his niece away. As to the future——' He shrugged and made a little slashing gesture across his throat.

'And we ride for Westminster to wait upon events.' Cranmer bowed his head as they paced away.

The King rode with them. His eyes sunk within circles of reddened flesh, his mouth a tight and bitter line, he sat his horse like some being of stone. None dared to speak to him or to look their pity.

At a window above the courtyard, the Queen stood whimpering, beating with her small fists upon the glass. It was quite useless, for she was too far away to make herself heard, and in any event she had already screamed herself hoarse up and down the corridor, crying over and over the King's name.

Henry would understand for he, of all men, loved her and had been kind to her. If he had not been the King she might have been able to confide in him, might have made him see through her eyes the loneliness of her childhood, the tawdriness of the big house with its echoing dormitories and the maids of honour who giggled secrets and stole the keys and let the young men up the back stairs when the old Duchess was in bed. But he had been the King, and she had been the Queen, and between them the truth must never be told.

Only now she was frightened, more frightened than she had ever been in her life before. Her whole body quivered and shook as if she had the ague and her heart beat violently in her breast. Her legs trembled as she ran down the passage and called imploringly, the bright spears of the guards dancing before her eyes, her own voice rising higher and higher into hysteria as she struggled to pass that barricade of shining steel.

But they had dragged her away and she had torn herself free and run again, to the other end of the corridor. The window there framed her small white face with its large green eyes, her disordered red hair, her small fists beating against the panes.

But the King and his Council rode away without looking back.

❉❉ CHAPTER FOURTEEN ❉❉

The Queen had put on one of her most becoming gowns as if in some pathetic way she hoped to charm the Archbishop. But Cranmer would not have noticed her attire if she had been sprayed in diamonds. He stood, miserably conscious of his duty, before her small, defiant figure and spoke gravely and kindly.

'It is of no use to deny these matters, Your Grace. We have evidence, freely offered, and substantiated by witnesses.'

'No, my lord, I am innocent,' she said stubbornly.

'Master Derham has made full confession, Madam, that you have lain with him.'

'No!' She twisted her hands together and repeated, 'No! Master Derham is a liar. What he says is not true; not true.'

'Is it not?' His sad gaze caught and searched her.

'No, no, no!' She caught her underlip between her teeth as her voice shrilled up.

'Madam, your guilt is clear and your life is forfeit according to the law,' Cranmer said sternly. 'But the King extends his gracious mercy to you. He believes that your sins were committed in ignorance. If you acknowledge them and make confession, you will not suffer.'

'I thank the King for his mercy, for all his goodness,' she said.

'And are filled, I hope, with a proper sense of contrition.'

'Indeed,' Katheryn cried earnestly, 'I'm very sorry if I have wronged him, for he has been kind to me.'

Cranmer stepped closer, his sonorous tones lending

dignity to his mild, stooping frame.

'Answer me now, Madam, truly and faithfully by the sacrament which you received on All Hallows—did you not lie with Master Derham?'

'He used—many times—to kiss me, sir,' she faltered. 'At night after my grandmother was in bed, the maids-in-waiting would steal the key and the young gentlemen of the household would creep up with wine and fruit. Master Derham came too and gave me sweetmeats.'

'And you lay with him?' Looking at her flushed face and downcast eyes he reminded her sternly, 'You are on holy oath, Madam.'

'I was constrained to it,' she said reluctantly.

'Yes?'

'Without my will or consent.' She gave him a sulky, pouting look.

'And you called him husband?'

'Perhaps. I don't remember. In jest people say many things.'

'But this was no jest. You were in fact promised to him.'

'To Derham?'

'You had precontract with him.'

'No. Never, sir,' she cried earnestly. 'My grandmother sent him from the house when she discovered what had befallen between us. And I was whipped, my lord, most cruelly whipped.'

'Madam, think now, I beg of you.' He was at his most persuasive and fatherly. 'I am trying to save Your Grace. If there was a precontract and you acknowledge it freely, then you are bigamous, but you may still be divorced.'

For a moment he thought she would seize the loophole, but then her head jerked up and her eyes gleamed coldly with all the pride of her blood.

'There was no precontract,' she said flatly. 'I am a

Howard, sir, and Master Derham a poor creature. I was foolish with him, yes, but he has not looked upon me nor touched me except in honour since I married with the King.'

'And for good reason which he has admitted,' Cranmer said.

'For what reason?' She cast him a swift, nervous look.

'Because when Derham came to Court he found that he was supplanted by another. That he had been succeeded in Your Grace's affections—by one, Thomas Culpepper.'

For a long moment she stared at him in silence. Then her face crumpled and she began to sob wildly, her fingers clutching his sleeve while words tumbled from her.

'Sir—of your goodness—help me. I beg you help me—for I would have wed him, but that they worked on me, sir, my lord of Norfolk, Bishop Gardiner, my grandmother, talking, whispering together, ever talking.'

'Of what? Talking of what?'

'Of the King's needing a new wife and England's needing a Catholic Queen. Over and over, saying he would give me jewels, saying I would be the first lady in the land. And so he did, sir, many jewels. And the people cheered me and bowed to me, and I had fine dresses. But Tom was here and so often with the King, and I could not forbear—but I was bound to the King, and now my fame is gone, and I am nothing young that I was, and I——'

She burst again into a fresh passion of weeping and he, moved by compassion, put out his hand towards her.

'Madam, you must calm yourself. You must be still.'

She swung away, her hands upraised as if to ward off a blow, her face contorted, her voice an ugly scream.

'Don't touch me! You all handle me, stroking me, beating the bedcurtain with the devil's wings until my flesh creeps with the horror of it. No, you're a good man, sir.' She clutched his hand, squeezing it tightly. 'It was she—my cousin, the Bullen—and they broke her neck. She died well, they say, nobly, but then she had Howard blood too.' Her eyes widened and her voice shrank to a whisper as she asked, 'What is it like to die, sir?'

He never knew afterwards what he had replied. He must have said something comforting, for he left her in a calmer frame of mind, crying quietly with her hands twisted in the rich stuff of her gown.

The Archbishop walked slowly, his head bent, his eyes fixed upon the ground. Poor, lightsome little Queen with her shallow mind and her greedy heart! Such women were victims of their own stupidity, and the cupidity of others. Yet they could inspire a devotion in others out of all proportion to their worth. Culpepper had not betrayed her even when the rack was stretched to its fullest extent. As for the King—the King hoped still to find some means of saving her. But then he knew nothing of Culpepper's part in the affair.

And it is I, Cranmer thought, who must put into His Grace's hands the document that will surely break his heart.

He did so privately in the King's chamber at Westminster where Henry had sat alone for most of each day since the investigations had begun. He had wept a great deal and eaten little so that there was about him, despite his bulk, an impression of a shrivelled being.

Cranmer handed over the document in silence and withdrew to the other end of the apartment where he stared unseeingly through the window. Behind him he could hear the faint rustling of paper and then the King's voice rose up into a bellow of anger and agony.

'Culpepper? Thomas? Thomas Culpepper? *No!*'

The word was the Queen's death sentence, but at that moment the Archbishop could feel pity only for the man who sat, digesting the knowledge that the woman he adored and the man he had treated as a son had made of him a cuckold.

On a cold, February day, with a hint of rain stinging the air, the Queen of England was led out to the place where her cousin had nobly died. The Bullen had died alone, bravely jesting with eyes so bright that for pity's sake they had hidden the sword in the straw and struck off her head without warning.

A sword for Nan wielded by an expert from Calais, and the dignity of a lonely death. For her little cousin the clumsy axe and the company of Lady Rochford, condemned as accomplice, and now, blank-eyed and unresisting, sunk into the apathy of madness.

Katheryn had passed from her own hysteria into a calm, even gentle frame of mind. The King loved her and so the King would pardon her. She kept that hope firmly in her mind even while, at her own request, the axe and block were brought to her room so she could rehearse the scene to be enacted the following day.

It would never really happen, of course! She would never fit her neck into the smooth hollow nor stretch out her arms in the traditional signal. It couldn't happen when she was not yet twenty and had all her life to live.

Those who watched the small, black-clad figure, marvelled at the composure of the young voice.

'I die as Queen of England, but I would liefer have died as the wife of Tom Culpepper.'

The King had ridden out hawking as he had done every morning since the Queen's arrest. It seemed as if he could not get sufficient kills, for though every day heaps of blood-stained feathers marked his trail he was out again the next dawn with his most savage hawk on his gauntleted wrist. The Court followed at a discreet distance, keeping their voices low, their expressions carefully blank.

These were strangely silent hawking expeditions with none of the laughter and jesting and cries of triumph that had marked other similar outings in the past. There was only the thudding of hoofs over the half-frozen ground and the beating of wings in the still air. Then came the swift descent, the outstretched talons and eager beak, the high scream from the smaller bird below. And another heap of bloodstained feathers lay upon the earth, red as a thornless rose.

Grey-faced, hard-eyes, with every line of every year etched upon his face, Henry sat his mount, watching with bitterness the slaughter of the innocent, but there were no innocent. He knew this now, and despised himself for the longings that swelled in him when he lay in his canopied bed, and knew that, when he put out his hand, it would meet not the soft shape of a woman but the emptiness of space.

He had found a little comfort in the unobtrusive friendship of the Archbishop and of Edward Seymour, who had taken over many of the routine cares of state.

Thomas Seymour was back at Court, too, a handsome, dare-devil with a reckless manner that reminded Henry of himself when young. The King had noticed him conversing earnestly with a lady in deep mourning.

'The Lady Latimer,' Cranmer nodded. 'She was formerly Catherine Parr. A cultured and elegant woman, sir.'

'For whom does she wear weeds? Her husband, I suppose.'

'She is twice widowed, sir. Her husbands were older than she was.'

'What age is she?'

'About thirty, Your Grace, but she has always been

grave and serious for her years. She is very fond of Prince Edward. I have seen her reading with him and amusing him.'

'A lady of good character, then?'

'Impeccable, sir,' Cranmer assured him. 'She was a most loyal and dutiful wife to both her lords, caring for them in their sickness.'

'She has kind eyes,' Henry said absently.

Fine eyes in a woman could lend distinction to the plainest face, and Lady Latimer had not a plain face. It had been a smooth, pretty one with tiny laughter lines about the mouth and eyes and an upward curve to the lips.

He had seen little of her shape under the concealing black robes, but he carried away in his mind an impression of plumpness and charm.

Katheryn had been more slender with an elasticity in her step that the Lady Latimer lacked. Perhaps she had lost it after tending two elderly husbands. That face had been designed for merriment.

His own face stiffened again into rigidity. Cursed be all Howard women, red-haired and black-haired, slant-eyed and slim-hipped. There was a poison in them all that drained away a man's vitality, made him trusting and feeble.

He had ordered Norfolk from Court, unable to bear the sight of the darkly subtle face, the ringed hands. Norfolk was a badly frightened man, having brought two nieces to the King's attention and both of them false. I have never, thought Henry with a surge of self-pity, really chosen a bride for myself.

Katherine was my brother's widow, forced upon me by my father that he might retain the Spanish dowry. Anne of Cleves was wished upon me by Cromwell and the Protestant League. Even my sweet Jane was brought to Court by her brothers that I might value her crystal innocence against the tawdry glamour of the Boleyn. And now I am old, more in need of a nurse than a wife.

His leg had begun to discharge again offensively. Sometimes he opened his mouth to bawl for Culpepper. Young Tom had been the only one who could dress the wound so that for a little while it ceased to throb. But Culpepper's head rotted now on Tower Bridge and it seemed to Henry that his own body mouldered too, as if one decay begat the other.

He narrowed his eyes, watching the graceful, deadly, circling hawk, feeling a sick satisfaction as the talons pierced the neck of the smaller bird. Kill or be killed, betray or be betrayed, hurt without mercy or have the heart torn out of you with longing.

Some distance away Suffolk and Seymour watched their monarch. In both their faces was an unwonted gentleness, for they had had no love for the flippant Queen, and their sympathy lay with the King who had been brother-in-law to both.

'His Grace needs a new wife,' Suffolk reflected now.

'Surely——' Edward Seymour gave the other a pained glance.

'Cranmer agrees with me. The best course of action when one is flung from a horse is to climb immediately up to another mare.'

'Would it be so easy now to find a lady willing to become Queen of England?' Seymour wondered.

'There is always a lady willing to become Queen of England,' the Duke said cynically, 'but I agree the choice must be a careful one.'

'A widow, perhaps? Someone used to the vagaries of an elderly husband.'

'And one inclined towards the Protestant Cause. We do not want Norfolk creeping back to favour.'

'But she ought not to be old,' Suffolk said. 'The King will not take a wife who is incapable of childbearing.'

'A well-educated woman who can share His Grace's interest in art and theological dissertation.'

'A comely woman who knows how to dress and behave so that she remains attractive without incurring the faintest breath of scandal.'

The two companions nodded at each other in respectful understanding. Then Suffolk frowned, staring past Edward Seymour to the cloaked figure who was approaching on horseback.

'For what reason does the Spanish Ambassador join the hawking party?' he wondered irritably.

'Perhaps he hopes for a cure for his gout,' Seymour said wryly.

'More likely he wishes an audience of His Grace. These foreigners have no tact.'

As he spoke the Duke wheeled his mount slantwise across the path of the Ambassador. Chapuys, looking cold and blue-tinged under the frosty sky, reined in his own mount and doffed his cap with an air of humouring mad Englishmen who rode out on a bitter morning instead of staying sensibly by the fire.

'I did not realise Your Excellency was of a sporting turn of mind,' Suffolk gibed.

'I am not, my lord. It is business, not pleasure, that brings me out. I find little amusement in the snaring of small animals and birds.'

'You prefer the torture of heretics, perhaps?' Seymour, who had joined them, spoke with deep distaste.

'That is not sport, my lord. That is religion.' Chapuys gave them a sly, worldly glance. 'I came on urgent business. I must have speech with His Grace.'

'That's quite impossible,' Suffolk said firmly. 'His Grace will not hear of business. He diverts himself in the field these thirty days.'

'While his Council rules the realm?' A thin Spanish eyebrow was raised.

'His Grace has complete confidence in his Council,'

Seymour said stiffly. 'And his present state of mind is such that——'

'Yes, yes. He mourns for the little Faithless Queen.' Chapuys flapped his gloved hand impatiently. 'Meanwhile there are affairs of state to be managed.'

'His Grace is not to be troubled by matters of state.'

'Nevertheless he will have to know that France has broken the peace and attacks the Emperor in his lands.'

The Ambassador nodded curtly and spurred his horse towards the solitary, brooding figure.

Later, in Council, the King sat like one wakening gradually out of a deep sleep while the Ambassador, looking a little warmer now, poured out the tale of French treachery.

'Your Grace must see that it is imperative you mobilise your ships for invasion,' he concluded.

'If I make war on France, I shall lose their annual tribute,' Henry said. 'Is the Emperor prepared to recompense me?'

'But, sir, you have already agreed with His Imperial Highness to campaign against the common enemy,' the Ambassador protested.

'How do I know that he will keep *his* word?' Henry asked blankly. 'I have been cheated too often, Signor. I am quite independent. If people want my help they must come forward with offers.'

'But Your Majesty——' Chapuys spread out his hands imploringly.

A cry from the garden outside diverted their attention. Through the window could be seen the white-suited figure of a boy of six. At this moment the white tunic was grimed and the child's mouth was open in a roar of indignation and pain. A small young lady, pacing with book in hand, had run towards the child, but another lady had reached him first and knelt, in a swirl of black garments, drawing him into her arms.

Her voice, gaily chiding, came to them faintly.

''Tis only a scratch, Your Grace, and princes must bear a few hurts if they insist on climbing trees.'

'Is His Highness in pain?' That was Mary's anxious tone.

'In great pain,' Lady Latimer said firmly, 'but he endures it most bravely as a Tudor must. We will go indoors and put witch-hazel upon it, and bind it firmly, and hunt for a sugarplum.'

'Your Grace must see that in honour you cannot draw back from your commitment with His Imperial Highness,' Chapuys was saying earnestly. 'If France overcomes the Empire she will turn all her resources against England.'

'I will think on the matter.'

The King's gaze was still fixed upon the window through which three forms could be seen moving away.

'If it is a question of terms——'

'I have said that I will think on it.' Henry's voice was sharp. 'I have other affairs to occupy me, apart from these foreign quarrels. We will talk again in a day or two.'

His eyes sought the window again, as his hand went up, unconsciously, to tidy his beard.

THE TIME OF THE DOVE

❉❉❉

CHAPTER FIFTEEN

It was chilly in the great apartment despite the heat of the fire. Catherine rubbed her numbed fingers and shivered a little. The two golden rings on her left hand glowed red in the light of the flames.

Two rings, two marriages. Her first had been made at the age of twelve and she had had stepchildren older than herself. But her husband had been kind and affectionate even if he was so often sick, and she had learned to mute her voice and her footsteps, to measure out physic, to sit for hours in a darkened room listening to the ramblings of an old man sliding rapidly into his second childhood.

When he was dead she had been married again to another old man. And he too had been kind and her stepchildren had loved her, and the disciplines of her first marriage had been invaluable in her second. She had been truly sorry when Lord Latimer had died, apart from the fact that she had had to go back into widow's weeds. Sometimes it felt as if she had been wearing black all her life.

And then she had come to Court and a man there had not cared that she was past thirty or that her face was pale through nights of watching by sickbeds. He had swaggered into the quietness of her life and taught her to laugh again and to talk nonsense. She remembered with desire his hard mouth pressed down upon hers and his arms holding her tightly with all a young man's yearning.

But it didn't do to allow her thoughts to roam down that path at such a moment. If what Archbishop Cranmer had hinted was true then she would need all her wits and all her courage if she were not to lose for ever the only opportunity of happiness she had ever known.

The King had limped into the room and she sank into a formal curtsey, her face bent as she rearranged her thoughts. When she rose he was looking at her in a friendly fashion and his voice was pleasant.

'We understand that you spend a good deal of time with our children, Lady Latimer. That you have become in their eyes a kind of unofficial governess.'

'They have been kind enough to admit me to their friendship, Your Grace,' she said shyly.

'And you enjoy their company?'

'Oh, yes, sire.' Her face lit into its charming smile. 'The Lady Mary is nearer to my own age, of course, so that we can discuss many matters together, but Lady Elizabeth is one of the brightest children I have ever known.'

'And Edward? What of the Prince?'

'His Grace is also very advanced,' she said slowly, 'but growing boys need exercise and fresh air. I have taken the liberty of encouraging him to spend as much time as possible in the garden, or with his pony. He already has a fine seat and sensitive hands.'

She paused, aware that nervousness was making her chatter too much. Then she heard the King, warmer and more informal.

'Your Ladyship likes children, I think.'

'I am not unused to them, sir,' she said primly, and a dimple showed briefly in her cheek.

'Since your husband's death I have seen you often at Court, Madam,' he remarked, 'and your house is noted for its entertainment.'

'My husband left me well-provided, sir.'

'He was an elderly man, I believe.'

'Both my husbands were elderly, Your Grace. Both were good men, and kind to me.'

'You spent your time quietly?'

'Very quietly, sir. I have always loved to read, however, so it didn't pass slowly when I had my books.'

'You favour the new faith, Madam, do you not?'

He poured wine into two goblets and handed her one, giving her a keen glance over the rim. Catherine sipped the drink carefully, trying to find the words that would express her own principles without bringing down upon herself the wrath of the King.

'I favour toleration, sir,' she said at last. 'I would give all men freedom of conscience, for I believe that God gave each man a conscience that he might be guided by it.'

'Many Protestants visit at your house, Madam, among them the Seymours.' Henry set down his goblet and stared at her from under his bushy brows. 'You are acquainted with Sir Thomas Seymour.'

'With him and his brother, sir.'

'Has Thomas Seymour been paying advances to you?' he barked.

'He pays advances to every lady under fifty,' Catherine said lightly, and drank the rest of her wine very carefully.

'Are you promised to him?' The voice was so mild that she was tempted to answer honestly, but some shifting light at the back of the King's eyes made her pause. There had been another young man called Thomas whose head still stared from Tower Bridge, and once he too had loved where a monarch desired.

'No, sir. I am not promised to him,' she said at last. 'I am a widow, sir, a mature woman and I have little interest in the frolics of a boy.'

'I,' said Henry, 'am a widower, and also unpromised.'

'We grieve for Your Majesty,' she said in a low voice, and wished the wine had warmed her more.

'We have made enquiries about you,' Henry said stiffly. 'I know you for a lady of good fame—serious and learned, Madam, you have that reputation. In short, we wish to wed with you.'

He brought the last words out harshly, gruffly, and cleared his throat.

It was what Cranmer had warned might happen, but she had refused to believe in the reality of it. Now the reality overcame her and she sank to her knees with an imploring, 'Your Majesty.'

'Well?' He gave her a hard stare curiously mingled with embarrassment.

'Your Majesty would find me ill-chosen for a wife,' she stammered.

'Why?'

Why could she not say fearlessly that she was in love with Thomas Seymour, that they were secretly pledged? There was nothing to prevent her—nothing save the shifting gleam at the back of the King's eyes, and the memory of a young head rotting on Tower Bridge.

'On account of my beliefs,' she said.

'You think them so different?' he asked in surprise.

'By your pardon, sir——'

'Yes?'

She wished he would stop interrupting and give her time to marshall her words. But she plunged on, reckless now.

'When a boy of fifteen can be tied to the stake at Smithfield, and burnt alive——'

'For speaking against the Holy Sacrament. That is a sin, Madam, and to condone it would be a greater sin.'

'Then I must be a great sinner, sir, and no fit mate for Your Grace,' she cried boldly.

'It is your woman's heart that makes you pity,' he excused her. 'Get up, Madam, do. I would not have you kneel to me. I am not angered by your opinions. It is your maternal tenderness that makes you so full of sympathy.'

'But I am not a mother, Your Grace.' Catherine

scrambled to her feet and stood, frantically twisting the rings on her hands. 'I have never borne a babe. After all these years of barrenness I am unlikely to bear one now. I doubt if I could give Your Majesty any children.'

'I already have a family, and they need a home,' he cut in. 'You said you enjoyed their friendship, but it is *your* friendship that they need. Edward and Elizabeth never knew their mothers, and Mary is old before her time.'

'I would always be their friend,' she said helplessly. 'I have not spoken of my own feelings.'

Henry turned away slightly, wincing as his weight pressed upon his leg, and Catherine, instinctively out of long habit was at once at his side, offering her shoulder, concern in her face.

'I desire company, Madam,' he said at last. 'I would not be alone; not alone.'

Suddenly she was no longer afraid of him, no longer revolted by the stench that rose from his leg. He was, after all, in need of comfort. He was sick and old and more than a little afraid, and she had a duty to the Protestant faith. Cranmer had told her that. But more than conscience was the pity welling up in her. She never had been able to resist another's needs.

'When I was a very little girl,' she said at last, 'a fortune-teller told me that one day I should be a Queen. After that I used to wonder when it would be and how it would feel to wear a crown upon my head.'

And the crown will be heavy, her thoughts ran on as the King embraced her. And Thomas Seymour was a dream I dreamed once who now must be forgotten. I will have a husband again and he will be good to me, and I shall grow old without ever knowing what it was like to be really young.

Later, in the garden, she met Thomas Seymour and told him briefly that she was to wed with the King. It was like killing part of herself to cause the expression of incredulous misery on his face.

'You can't do it, Catherine. He's an old man. A brutal man.' He held her arm so tightly that she knew it would be bruised.

'He needs me,' she said.

'So do I! I need you,' he insisted. 'I've loved you ever since you came to Court. There'll be no other women for me.'

'You're young; you'll forget.'

'Never!' he vowed and his dark face flushed with anger and pride. 'Forget the only woman I ever loved? Do you think me so shallow? I'll wait for you, d'ye hear me? He won't live long, for he's rotted with the pox already, and when he's dead I'll come courting you.'

'Hush! It's ill-luck to speak of death.'

She held her hand to his mouth.

'And I'll love you while he lives. At least I can see you sometimes, touch your hand——'

'No!' She wrenched herself free, her composure gone, her breasts heaving under the black gown. 'I too have feelings,' she whimpered. 'Do you think that I could endure to be so near to you and not touch you, to feel your eyes upon me and not be able to meet your gaze? It would be intolerable. And dangerous.'

'I am not afraid of danger,' he boasted.

'For me,' she said swiftly. 'Dangerous for me. You must go away from Court, for a while at least, until I am settled in marriage with the King. For my sake, if you love me, you must do this for me.'

Her voice faltered and broke and then she was stepping away from him across the grass, with her coifed head high and a gallant tilt to her shoulders.

She was glad that he did not stay for the marriage, for it would have been unendurable to exchange vows under his hurt, resentful gaze. Thomas Seymour was a man who found relief in action and by the time he returned she would have learned to think of herself as the King's wife.

It would be a quiet wedding as befitted the joining together of two people past their first youth. As she stood in the private chamber of Hampton Court, dressed in her bridal robes, Catherine kept her mind firmly on small, unimportant details. The fur on the Archbishop's mantle was slightly rubbed, a sign of Cranmer's simplicity and lack of interest in material concerns.

'My dear child, remember that by this match you are helping to propound the Protestant faith,' he had said earnestly. 'And if ever you need advice I shall be only too happy to help you in any way that I can.'

Advise me now, Archbishop. Tell me how to rip out from my heart and brain the image of a dark face, the remembered touch of lips and hands, the echo of a mocking voice.

Mary was her female attendant. Catherine had asked that the King's elder daughter be allowed to come. It was possible, by slanting her gaze, to see the tense figure and to remind herself that this was the girl to whom the company of an affectionate, cultured stepmother would mean a great deal.

You are too self-controlled, my dear, and there is a bitterness in your eyes and around your mouth that should be softened by a smile. But you rarely smile and I have never heard you laugh. It will be different now. I will help you and you must help me. You must tell me about the others, tell me of the other women who stood as I stand now, giving their lives into the hands of this gross, lonely, terrifying old man.

The King glanced at Catherine.

She is like a small, white dove, he thought, gentle but capable of a furious pecking when someone she loves is in danger. Her hands are square and capable, the hands of a nurse; and there is a dimple in her cheek. It will be amusing to coax it out. Cranmer looks as grave as if he were conducting the funeral rite instead of the marriage service. I must twit him about it later. Suffolk, at least, looks festive. And young for his years, despite his bulk. But then he too married a young wife. I wonder if Catherine was right when she spoke of being barren. Her other husbands were impotent, I daresay.

For a moment his other weddings rushed up in his mind, and Catherine's figure blurred into other figures.

Katherine had been plump, too, her fair hair streaming down her back in token of her virginity. But that had been a lie, proved by the dead sons that marked nearly every year of their marriage; and she had grown withered and querulous with all her pomegranate promise sucked dry.

The Bullen wedding had been a secret, dawn affair. In the half-light Anne's narrow face with its slanting lids and pointed chin had had a strange, mystic quality. And that had been a deception, too, for he should have remembered that falcons were birds of prey.

Catherine had in her something of the still purity of Jane, but snowdrops never outlived their spring, and it was best not to disturb the green turf that spread itself above them.

An involuntary grin creased his cheeks when he thought of his bride from Cleves, so that the Archbishop raised a slightly pained eyebrow. Dear Flanders mare with her pock-marked face and perpetual smile!

How strange to look back now and recall his own horror at the bride. Now they were on the best of terms, for Anne's English had improved immeasurably and her house had become noted for the excellence of its cuisine.

She had been unconventional enough to entertain him and Katheryn—but no! on this day he must not think of roses spilling their velvet petals to the ground, of roses crushed under a spiked heel into a shredded mass of pulped scarlet.

He closed his mind against the torment of memories and listened to the quiet voice at his side.

'I, Catherine, take thee, Henry, to my wedded husband, to have and to hold from this day forward, for better for worse, for richer for poorer, in sickness and in health——'

Her cheek was round and smooth under his kiss and there were tears in her eyes. Women often wept at weddings, even their own, and it was natural that Catherine should be apprehensive. He felt a stirring of deep affection within him and his tone was jocular as he gripped Cranmer's hand.

'We will bring Prince Edward and the Lady Elizabeth to Hampton Court. They will be company for Her Grace when I am occupied with state affairs.'

'I hope you will not be absent from us too long at a time, sir,' Catherine said gracefully, and gained an approving nod from the Archbishop.

But there was no kindly prelate to smile encouragement when she stood, shivering and white-gowned with her long hair down her back, by the high canopied bed on which the King, night-robed and tasselcapped, was propped.

'You look younger than your years, Madam,' Henry observed, holding out his hand towards her.

Catherine put out her own hand to meet it and was startled by the dry, burning flesh. The exclamation rose spontaneously to her lips.

'You are not well, sir!'

'My leg pains me,' he admitted.

'Your Grace stood on it for too long a time,' she chided. 'And now it needs to be dressed again. I will send for bandages and salve, and make Your Grace more comfortable.'

'It is not a sight for a woman,' he objected.

'I am well-used to sick nursing,' she said gently, 'and I am your wife, sir. It is a wife's place to tend her husband and care for his children.'

'Out of duty?'

'Out of affection, sir,' she lied, and bent over the mass of pus-soaked bandages. The hot, heavy hand fell upon her hair tenderly and she closed her eyes against the pain and the pity that swept over her.

A few days later, the King, having doffed his honeymoon face and donned the mask of business, sat at the head of the long table and looked round at the members of his Council.

'It is our intention,' he said briskly, 'to leave the Queen as Regent during our absence in France. You will, I know, give Her Grace the full benefit of your advice and support.'

'Sir, is it your purpose to enter France in person?' Cranmer asked with a disapproving edge to his voice.

'It is,' Henry said shortly, and frowned as he noticed the covert glances cast about the table.

'We would beg Your Grace to consider the danger of such an undertaking,' Cranmer said.

'Are you still afraid of Scotland?' Henry demanded. 'Marie de Guise will not risk a Flodden field by invading while we are across the Channel. She knows very well that I would not leap into the sea and leave my back unguarded. You need not be afraid of Scotland.'

'Sir, we are more concerned for your own safety,' Suffolk said quickly, 'lest Your Majesty's life should be endangered.'

Henry's pouched eyes met the darker gaze of his old comrade, and a little thrill of anger quivered up his spine. He knew very well what they were all thinking but were too tactful to say. He was too old, too sick, too fat to ride into battle at the head of his army.

He heaved himself to his feet and tapped his way

down the length of the table, the veins on his forehead swelling with indignation.

'There's no danger in the French, Brandon. You know as well as I do that they run like armoured hares when they scent an enemy. Remember the Battle of the Spurs!'

He forced himself to laugh, to beat down their anxious eyes.

'Nevertheless it might be better for Your Grace to remain in this country,' Cranmer persisted.

'No, no, you shall not persuade me to stay home.'

He had meant to roar but his voice emerged feebly querulous. He raised it to still the pounding of blood in his ears.

'The Emperor is leading his army—I shall lead mine—my forces into——'

The floor had begun to tilt towards the ceiling. He stumbled against the table and went down heavily on one knee. He was aware that people were starting to their feet, that Suffolk and Cranmer were bending over him. He waved them away feebly, exerting his last strength, leaning his head against the table as visions of the past flooded his throbbing brain.

He was a golden youth, splendid in his strength and beauty, riding a fine horse down a narrow street with cheering people pressed close along the side. A girl with a mouth like a poppy reached up to hang a garland around his neck, and he swung her up to the saddle behind him, but his grasp was weak and old and the girl melted between his fingers, and his hair was not red but grey, and his ardent spirit was enclosed in stinking flesh.

Slowly, painfully, with infinite care, the King pulled himself to his feet, his knuckles swollen white against the edge of the table. Slowly, painfully, he forced the image of the golden youth out of his mind and looked, through the blurred and lonely eyes of an old man, at the alarmed and startled face of his Council.

'We will not go far.' His voice gained an echo of strength as he went on. 'I only care about taking Boulogne. We will fulfil our part of the bargain and invade the country; but no more.'

For a moment his lip jutted out like a sulky child.

'You need not fear, my lords,' he said with a pathetic dignity, 'that I will slow your marches.'

He remained on his feet as, one by one, the members of the Council made their bows and left. Nobody spoke, and there was in their silence some quality of loving that had survived the years.

Long after they had gone the Queen came into the great chamber on soft, sandalled feet and went to where the King sat in the high-backed chair, his hands clasped tightly around the top of his stave, his chin sunk upon his hands as if he brooded upon past glories too dim to remember clearly.

After a moment he raised his head and saw her standing there, her face grave under the silver coif, her own hands with their bands of gold clasped lightly one over the other.

'I shall go into France, Madam,' he said at last. 'I shall lead my armies into battle once more.'

'Your armies will expect it,' she said steadily.

'And you will remain as Regent. I have made that clear.'

'I will care for Your Grace's children too,' she said, domestic priorities uppermost in her mind.

'You are a good wife, Catherine,' he said at last.

'And have I not reason to be, sir?'

She moved to his side, slipping her arm expertly beneath his shoulder, assisting him to rise.

'We shall beat the French, you know. We always do,' he said confidently.

'Of course, sir, but I shall be glad to have you safe home again.'

'Oh, I shall come home again, never fear,' he asserted. 'The seasoned warrior always returns, and I am not old yet. I am not old, am I, Catherine?'

'No, sir.'

Gently, unobtrusively, she allowed him to lean upon her as they made their slow progress from the room.

❉❉ CHAPTER SIXTEEN ❉❉

The brothers stood together in the archway, their tall figures similar in build but contrasting in attitude, for Edward Seymour stood neatly as though preparing to deliver a brief in Council, while Thomas leaned negligently against the carved post as if, action over, he rested for a brief moment before, like some brilliant butterfly, he drifted to sample more succulent nectar.

The room itself was a symphony of autumn shades, red blended with brown merging into the gold of a leaf caught unawares in sunlight. Fires blazed like outbursts of laughter at both ends of the apartment and the air was rich with the perfume of apple logs lazily settling into their glowing beds of ash.

Another archway framed the royal family as if posed for some animated portrait group. Henry, his leg upon a footstool, leaned over the slighter figure of his son, his thick fingers setting the boy's child hands in the correct position on the lute he was teaching him to play. Upon the red full-moon face of the father and the green new-moon face of the son had fallen the intense concentration of two artists passionately absorbed in their art.

Near to them, coifed heads tilted to catch the notes of melody, Mary with the eager eyes and bitter mouth and Elizabeth with the eager mouth and bitter eyes sat together. Their hands were poised over silk threads half-drawn through their tapestry frames as though both feared the rasping whisper might disrupt the more potent threads of melody woven by Henry and Edward.

At the other side, the Queen sat, a little apart, her

hands brushing her skirt lightly over and over as if in some small gesture she could find release for unimaginable anguish. Her face wore a tender smile that had no connection with the restless, jewelled fingers, and her eyes were shadowed by the crescent lashes tipped golden by the firelight.

'He has found happiness of a sort,' Edward Seymour remarked in a low, satisfied undertone.

'Of a strange sort,' Thomas muttered, and the brilliant butterfly was suddenly a sinister and predatory moth drawn close to an innocent candle flame.

'It would be well for you to cast your eyes in another direction,' Edward warned. 'Her Grace is not invulnerable.'

'Do I not know it? I have not forgotten Mistress Askew,' Thomas returned.

They fell silent for a moment, smelling in imagination the roasting flesh and blazing hair, hearing in imagination the tortured screams of the woman who had once been beautiful but who, stretched upon the rack, had become no more than a twisted travesty of a human being.

Anne Askew had denied the Mass, had read forbidden books, had drawn about her a circle of influential ladies to discuss the new doctrines. *Very* influential ladies, the whisper had run, but Mistress Askew had not, even in her last extremity, named any of her friends.

But that had not prevented an accusation of heresy from being drawn up against the Queen. And the King had signed the warrant for her arrest. It was monstrous, unbelievable and the Council were still shaking their heads over it.

Henry's affection for his wife was, they would have sworn, both deep and genuine, and yet when the accusations against her had been presented to him he had penned his signature at the foot of the document.

The presentation of the warrant had, in fact, followed a slight coolness between the King and Queen, arising from what had begun as an attempt on Catherine's part to explain the logic of Lutheran belief and had ended with Henry angrily limping out, exclaiming that things had come to a pretty pass when a wife instructed her husband in theological matters.

But word of the existence of that signed warrant had filtered to the Queen's solar, and for a long morning the ladies had shivered in their shoes until Catherine, for the first time in her life, had lost her air of calm self-possession and screamed hysterically over and over.

Eventually Henry had been forced to enquire the reason for the uproar and that had been the excuse for Catherine to fling herself on her knees before him, begging to know the reason for his displeasure.

'Argue, sir? I but tried to take your mind off the pain in your leg. I wished to present my mind as the flint against which you could strike the flame of your sharper wit.'

And the King had forgiven her for being intelligent and kissed her and called her his sweet Cathy. And when Wriothesley had come later with the warrant, he had been yelled out of the royal presence.

An incident that might have become bloodstained had turned into farce, but it could have been very different. Nobody at Court ever forgot that. Catherine, above all, remembered the cold terror that had gripped her when she had seen the paper that condemned her to be burnt for her opinions. For that reason she walked warily now, with a gentle smile and downcast lashes.

She glanced up in the direction of the Seymours and the faint rose colour deepened in her cheeks. It was only for a moment, and then she rose, inclining her head slightly, as she spoke in her sweetly placid voice.

'His Highness already displays such skill that an audience has gathered. Will you not join us, sirs?'

'If His Grace consents to play one of his own compositions,' Edward Seymour said genially.

'My fingers are stiff,' Henry grumbled, but he took the lute from his son's grasp and an autumn melody rippled through the room.

Edward Seymour beat time softly with his foot, but the younger brother fixed his gaze moodily upon the Queen. Catherine, however, did not look at him again, but went over to the Lady Elizabeth and, holding the young girl as a shield between herself and danger, helped her to untangle the embroidery silks.

'We waste time,' Henry said at last, breaking off in the midst of a chord. 'I should be preparing my speech for the opening of Parliament.'

'I wish I could be there, sir,' Elizabeth exclaimed.

'Pooh! A woman who sat in a Parliament would be a strange sight,' Henry chaffed her. 'Ladies have neither the wit nor the stamina. It is for them to listen to their husbands, eh, Catherine?'

'Indeed, Your Grace, I have often profited from your instruction,' the Queen agreed demurely, 'but I must confess that I too would give much to hear Your Grace's words.'

'It will, I think,' said Henry with a certain complacency, 'be a Parliament to remember.'

So indeed it proved, for few of those who crowded into the packed Hall of Westminster that day were unaware of the frailty of the King's health, nor of the fact that this might be the last time any of them saw him again. They knelt in a close and sweating silence, their faces upturned to the crowned and robed figure on the daïs.

The King's voice, reedier now than in youth, was still powerful enough to reach the fringes of the gathering, and his eyes, roaming from member to member, held still a cold and terrible majesty.

'Trusty and well-beloved subjects, it is not unknown to you that we have reigned o'er this realm for nearly forty years, during which time we have so ordered, thanks be to God, that no outward enemy has oppressed you or taken anything from you.'

Forty years and each year strung on the chain of my life in dark and lighter stones. Forty years for the holding of an island, and the telling of a tale.

'Now it may be the last time we shall have occasion to prorogue this Parliament and address the Estates of our realm. I do therefore thank you for those subsidies you have voted for the war. Though we have been in some danger, our fleet, our fortresses have kept the French from these shores. But unless you, my lords temporal, and you, my lords spiritual, and you, my loving subjects, study to amend one thing which is amiss, there can be no peace *within* the realm.'

The lion's teeth are not yet drawn, so you may take that politely humouring look from your faces.

'Charity and concord are not among you. Saint Paul said, "Charity is gentle, Charity is not envious, Charity is not proud." But what love and charity is in you when one calls another heretic, papist, anabaptist? I am very sorry to know how unreverently the Word of God is disputed in every ale-house in the land. This kind of man is depraved and that. This ceremony and that ceremony. Such presumption must stop. No prince in the world favours his subjects more than I do, but you must amend these errors.'

All subjects must live in harmony with the conscience of the King, for I have followed my conscience all my life and it has brought me into a safe harbour.

'Be in charity one with another. Love, dread, and fear God, to which I, as your Supreme Head and Sovereign Lord, exhort and require you. And then I doubt not but that love and league, that I spoke of in the beginning, shall never be dissolved or broke between us.'

He had ended, after all, on a quiet note and, in that quietness, he drew his robes about him and limped slowly out, gathering up men's heart strings as he went.

It was over now, the golden youth was sunk into greyness and the splendour of a rising sun had mellowed into the glow of evening. And those who had seen it all from the beginning to the end let him make his way alone to the waiting attendants, for in that moment there was no man worthy to stand beside him.

I have been, Henry thought, as the vistas of his life receded, a great King, for I have held England safely in the hollow of my hand, and bent other princes to my will. And I have kept faith with my conscience which is as much as any man can do.

The walls of the room closed in about him, and he saw then that the room itself was crowded with people. The Council were there. He could recognise Wriothesley, Audley, Gardiner, the Seymours—but where were Thomas Wolsey, Thomas More and Thomas Cromwell? Dead, of course. Two by the axe, the other in the shadow of the axe. And Norfolk was in the Tower. If Henry could manage to survive until the morning, his kinsman would be led out to Tower Green, ostensibly for the treason of quartering his shield with the royal arms. But both he and the King knew that his real crime had been to push two nieces towards the royal marriage bed. For a second he could not remember if Cranmer had been executed or not.

'You will guard my son well,' he ordered weakly. 'Be loyal to him.'

He will need loyalty, that one legitimate male seed of my loins. There are greedy men in the kingdom waiting to tear it apart.

A stifled sob directed his attention to the small, bowed figure who waited near the bed. Mary, he thought wryly, was like Katherine of Spain in that she could not weep prettily but must needs blotch her face and redden her eyes and nose. Poor Mary had wept a great deal in her life, and not least for the lack of a husband and children.

To Mary he said the one thing that might comfort her.

'Mary, I pray you be a mother to him, for he is very little yet.'

She choked out a 'Yes, sire,' and moved away, her hands to her face.

Edward Seymour came forward in response to his monarch's lifted hand and stood, neat and solemn, his hands clasped within his sleeves.

'As his uncle you will be Lord Protector.' Henry felt, rather than heard, the little gasps at this new title. 'The succession will go to the Prince, then to the Princess Mary, then to the Lady Elizabeth.'

It was too late to argue about the legality or otherwise of their mothers' marriages. He had bastardised and legitimised his two daughters so often that even he was not certain exactly where they stood at that particular moment. In any event it mattered little, for Edward would marry and beget sons of his own. Edward *must* marry, else the striving would all have been in vain.

'Are the French and Imperial Ambassadors at hand?' he remembered to ask.

'Yes, sir.'

'I will give them audience,' he began, but the Council were whispering together, shaking their heads, and he was too weary to repeat the command.

Then Edward Seymour leaned closer to the pillow.

'Your Grace must prepare to meet his God,' he said, low yet clear.

'What judge sends you to pass this sentence?' Henry heard himself say.

'Your physicians, sir. They can do no more.'

He respected the other's courage, for he knew it was no easy thing to tell a King that he must die. In choosing Seymour as Lord Protector he had chosen wisely.

'And there's the one honesty,' he said. 'The one truth in an uncertain world.'

Someone brought him wine and he sipped gratefully, catching the Queen's eyes over the rim of the goblet. Poor Catherine had nursed him so patiently.

'Madam,' he said gently, 'it is God's will that we should part and I order all these gentlemen to treat you as if I were living still.'

It was a last tribute to her faithfulness, and it touched him to see the Council bow towards her in recognition of her position.

'Will Your Grace make confession now?' Gardiner was asking.

'To Cranmer,' he murmured. 'But not yet. First I would sleep a little.'

And dream of the golden youth who rode a white charger, of the girl with a mouth like a poppy, of a falcon swooping from the sky upon a laughing rose. But his mind was empty of all dreams, all memories, save one of a girl walking in a meadow and stooping now and then to pluck the blossoms.

'For my body—let it be laid to rest at Windsor,' he instructed.

'Yes, Your Grace.'

'With her. With Jane.'

He sent a long, apologetic look towards the Queen, and Catherine nodded slowly and moved into the shadow as if the living gave place, at this moment, to the more deeply-loved dead.

A single tear fell from the King's eye and then both

his eyelids fluttered down.

Faintly he heard Cranmer's voice, felt his hand taken in a cool, dry grasp.

'Your Grace—do you die in the faith of Christ?'

There was so much to be said, and he was too tired.

'Do you die in Christ's faith, sire?' the voice asked again.

The royal hand pressed down upon Cranmer's knuckles, then, slowly as a sigh, relaxed, and the King had gone.

The Archbishop crossed himself and glanced towards Seymour who moved with grave measured tread towards the antechamber where lesser members of the Court waited; where the new monarch clung weeping to his half-sister.

The herald's voice echoed from stone to stone.

'Of your charity, pray for the soul of the most High and Mighty Prince, our late Sovereign Lord, King Henry the Eighth.'

And after that there was silence.

BB
STANLEY KUBRICK'S
CLOCKWORK ORANGE